PALOS VERDES LIBRARY DISTRICT

S0-BCZ-760

JUN 1 0 2021
Palos Verdes Library District

R.
Verdes Library District

DOG
SQUAD

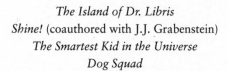

FAVORITES FROM CHRIS GRABENSTEIN

The Island of Dr. Libris
Shine! (coauthored with J.J. Grabenstein)
The Smartest Kid in the Universe
Dog Squad

MR. LEMONCELLO'S LIBRARY SERIES

Escape from Mr. Lemoncello's Library
Mr. Lemoncello's Library Olympics
Mr. Lemoncello's Great Library Race
Mr. Lemoncello's All-Star Breakout Game
Mr. Lemoncello and the Titanium Ticket

WELCOME TO WONDERLAND SERIES

Home Sweet Motel
Beach Party Surf Monkey
Sandapalooza Shake-Up
Beach Battle Blowout

HAUNTED MYSTERY SERIES

The Crossroads
The Demons' Door
The Zombie Awakening
The Black Heart Crypt

COAUTHORED WITH JAMES PATTERSON

Best Nerds Forever
The House of Robots series
The I Funny series
The Jacky Ha-Ha series
Katt vs. Dogg
The Max Einstein series
Pottymouth and Stoopid
Scaredy Cat
The Treasure Hunters series
Word of Mouse

CHRIS GRABENSTEIN

ILLUSTRATIONS BY BETH HUGHES

RANDOM HOUSE 🏠 NEW YORK

This is a work of fiction. Names, characters, places, and incidents either are the product of the author's imagination or are used fictitiously. Any resemblance to actual persons, living or dead, events, or locales is entirely coincidental.

Text copyright © 2021 by Chris Grabenstein
Jacket art and interior illustrations copyright © 2021 by Beth Hughes

All rights reserved. Published in the United States by Random House Children's Books, a division of Penguin Random House LLC, New York.

Random House and the colophon are registered trademarks of Penguin Random House LLC.

Photo on p. 310 © *New York Daily News* Archive/Susan Watts

Visit us on the Web! rhcbooks.com

Educators and librarians, for a variety of teaching tools, visit us at RHTeachersLibrarians.com

Library of Congress Cataloging-in-Publication Data
Names: Grabenstein, Chris, author. | Hughes, Beth, illustrator.
Title: Dog Squad / Chris Grabenstein; illustrations by Beth Hughes.
Description: First edition. | New York: Random House Children's Books, [2021] | Series: Dog Squad; 1
Summary: "Fred, a scrappy and lovable dog, gets cast as a stand-in for the lead role in *Dog Squad,* a show about crime-fighting dogs, and he soon finds out the action doesn't always stop on-screen"— Provided by publisher.
Identifiers: LCCN 2020034910 | ISBN 978-0-593-30173-9 (trade) | ISBN 978-0-593-30174-6 (lib. bdg.) | ISBN 978-0-593-42559-6 (int'l ed.) | ISBN 978-0-593-30175-3 (ebook)
Subjects: CYAC: Dogs—Fiction. | Adventure and adventurers—Fiction. | Television—Production and direction—Fiction.
Classification: LCC PZ7.G7487 Dog 2021 | DDC [Fic]—dc23

Printed in Canada
10 9 8 7 6 5 4 3 2 1
First Edition

Random House Children's Books supports the First Amendment and celebrates the right to read.

Penguin Random House LLC supports copyright. Copyright fuels creativity, encourages diverse voices, promotes free speech, and creates a vibrant culture. Thank you for buying an authorized edition of this book and for complying with copyright laws by not reproducing, scanning, or distributing any part in any form without permission. You are supporting writers and allowing Penguin Random House to publish books for every reader.

FOR BROADWAY ANIMAL TRAINERS BILL AND
DOROTHY BERLONI, WHO RESCUED OUR FRED
AND HAVE FOUND SO MANY LOVING HOMES
FOR SO MANY LUCKY DOGS

1

NALA, THE WORLD'S bravest and boldest border collie, bounded through the brambles.

"The river just jumped its banks, Duke," she reported. "We need to herd it back to where it belongs!"

"You can't herd water!" said Scruffy, his wiry whiskers twitching. "That's harder than herding cats!"

"Well, we need to do something," said the steely-eyed Duke. "Because the Wilkins farm is directly downstream!"

"The Wilkins farm?" shrieked Scruffy. "Their new puppies will be swept away in the flood!"

"Oh no they won't," said Duke.

"Not on our watch!" added the noble Nala.

"When trouble calls"—Duke arched his left eyebrow heroically—"it's Dog Squad to the rescue!"

Nala barked.

Scruffy yapped.

Duke took off running.

"Follow me!" he shouted over his shoulder.

The three dogs raced alongside the swollen river. The music was very dramatic, with lots of DUN-DEE-DUN-DUN-DUNs. It was the kind of music that made a chase scene even more exciting.

"There!" said Nala, focusing her laser-sharp eyes and pointing. "In the rapids! Six puppies!"

"I've heard of giving dogs a bath," cracked Scruffy, "but this is ridiculous."

"Dog Squad!" shouted a weeping mother dog on the far shore of the river. "Help! Save my children! They're in trouble!"

"Don't worry, ma'am," boomed Duke over the roar

of the raging rapids. "No harm shall befall your pups. Not today. We're the Dog Squad." He gazed toward the horizon. Wind tousled his fur just so. The sun glinted off his eyes. "And we're going in after them!"

"We are?" said Scruffy. "Those rapids look pretty, you know, *rapid,* Duke."

"That just means we'll get downstream faster!"

Duke leapt into the water.

"Pawsome!" cried Nala as she jumped in behind Duke.

Scruffy sighed. "Nothing's too ruff for us!" He sprang off the rocky riverbank and belly-flopped into the churning stream below.

Grunting hard and flexing every muscle he had to flex, Duke fought his way to the middle of the whitecapped water. Muddy waves crested, dragging along branches torn from trees upstream.

"Help!" peeped an adorable puppy, bobbing up and down in the water. "Help!"

"Hang on, son!" shouted Duke. "We're coming."

"Duke!" cried Scruffy. "There's only three of us but six of them. We can't possibly save 'em all."

"Oh yes we can, Scruffy. We're the Dog Squad."

"Saving puppies is what we do best!" added Nala.

"But how?" gurgled Scruffy, spitting out a mouthful of dirty water.

Duke could see all six puppies. Three were flailing.

Two were frantically treading water. One was biting a stick like it was a chew toy.

"Of course!" said Duke. "Bite onto a couple of those branches, gang. I'll strip some bark off this log. We'll lash together a raft and float these puppies home!"

LIKE DOGS ALL across America, Fred was glued to his human's TV, watching the new episode of *Dog Squad* that had just started streaming that night.

Fred loved the heart-racing, tail-wagging adventures of Scruffy, Nala, and their fearless leader, Duke!

All the dogs in the show were voiced by human actors, of course, because even though dogs could talk among themselves, they still hadn't cracked the code for human speech.

"Hop aboard, sport!" Duke called to the last puppy still furiously paddling in the swirling water alongside the raft Fred's heroes had just lashed together.

"My name's Rocko, not Sport," the puppy snapped back.

Fred laughed. On-screen, Duke chuckled the way all heroes chuckle as he plucked Rocko out of the river. Then he gave the little guy an ear nuzzle that made the puppy giggle.

Awwww, thought Fred.

It was one of those cute *awwww* moments that *Dog Squad* always did right after its action scenes. Fred loved the *awwww* moments. And the action scenes. He loved EVERYTHING. The whole show.

Fortunately, Fred's owner, Big Tony Bomboloni, wasn't home most Thursday nights, when fresh episodes came online. Big Tony wouldn't want to watch *Dog Squad,* because Big Tony didn't really like dogs. He'd only adopted Fred from the animal shelter because he thought that, with enough harsh training, Fred could become a guard dog—the super-aggressive kind that Big Tony could sell to the highest bidder.

Big Tony was always trying to get rich quick.

Just the other week, he bent all his refrigerator magnets and tried to sell them online as miracle medical bracelets to gullible senior citizens.

Fred frowned thinking about it.

If Big Tony was on *Dog Squad,* the good guys would catch him, lock him up, and throw away the key. It was too bad that justice wasn't as swift or fair in real life as it was on *Dog Squad.*

Truth was, Fred just wasn't cut out to be a guard dog. He wanted to be part of a forever family, not a money-making scheme. A real family. Like he'd almost had with Susan.

Fred sighed. Whenever he thought of Susan, he remembered long walks in the park, cozy cuddle time on the couch, and a bowl that was always filled with kibble.

Susan had loved Fred. She even gave him his name. F-R-E-D. Wrote it on his collar in big, bold strokes. But then Susan fell in love with Mike, and Mike thought Fred was a mutt (he was). Mike didn't want to be seen walking a mutt in New York City's Central Park.

If they were going to get married, Mike told Susan, Fred had to go. If Susan needed a dog, Mike said he would buy her a new one—a purebred from a trainer he knew about in Pennsylvania. Purebreds made much more fashionable canine companions. Susan agreed. Because she was more in love with Mike than she had been with Fred.

Three weeks before their wedding, Susan took Fred to an animal shelter on East 110th Street, where she told a whole bunch of lies, including "My fiancé is allergic to him."

Fred blinked hard. Sometimes it was so sad to think about Susan.

"Duke!" shouted Nala on the TV. Her eyes narrowed. She was focused on something rising up behind the raft.

Oh no! Fred saw it, too. A towering wall of water.

"The beaver dam upstream," said Nala, somehow

keeping her cool the way she always did. "It must've burst. Here comes a tsunami!"

"Cowabunga, everybody!" Duke scooped up all the puppies, tucked three under each arm, and stood on his hind legs to ride the rickety raft like a surfboard on the crest of a thirty-foot wave.

It was so cool! Fred wished he could do it too! He wished he could be like Duke!

"When trouble calls," Fred said in his best Duke voice, "it's Dog Squad to the rescue!"

He leapt up on the ratty sofa in Big Tony's basement TV room as if it was the raging river. He pretended the cushions were puppies in need of rescuing.

"Saving puppies is what we do best! Nothing's too ruff for us! We're pawsome!"

Fred plucked up the cushions, one by one, and tossed them to safety on the floor.

He was rescuing a throw pillow, thrashing it back and forth to free it from a tangle of imaginary vines, when he heard the cellar steps creaking.

He froze.

Fred knew what the creaking steps meant.

Big Tony had come home early!

"WHAT THE HECK do you think you're doing?" Big Tony shouted at Fred.

Fred tucked his tail between his legs and dropped his eyes. Big Tony had pasty skin, oily black hair, and angry, beady eyes.

"That couch cost me twenty-five bucks! Do you have twenty-five bucks? No. Because you're nothing but a lazy moocher!"

Big Tony grabbed Fred by his raggedy collar.

"What was I thinking?" snarled Big Tony. "A stray like you could never become a guard dog! You're afraid of everything! Even thunder!"

He dragged Fred up the steps to the first floor.

He threw open the apartment's back door and tossed Fred out into the alley.

"Get out and stay out! You no-good, miserable mutt!

I can't believe I wasted my time trying to train you! And don't come back, neither!"

The door slammed shut.

Fred's spirits sank. He wasn't surprised by what had just happened. Big Tony had told him, over and over, that he was useless, that he'd never be mean or tough enough to be a real guard dog. It was true. One time, Fred saw a pair of mice in the kitchen. He didn't chase them away. He just watched them nibble the chunk of cheese that had fallen out of Big Tony's sandwich. The mice were hungry.

And now, so was Fred. He was starving.

Without a home, will I ever eat again?

The thought rumbled through Fred's head as hunger grumbled through his belly. Big Tony hadn't fed Fred lately. His only supper had been a pair of half-chewed pizza crusts he'd found on the kitchen floor.

Fred started up the alley, sniffing for familiar scents.

But it had rained recently. The smells had all been washed away.

What would Duke do? he wondered.

Easy! Duke would chase down a dog food delivery truck! Then he'd jump up on its rear bumper, work open the doors with his snout, and help himself (not to mention Scruffy and Nala) to a dog food feast. He'd also repay the kindly truck driver by saving their life when their gas pedal got stuck to the floor.

Yep. That was what Duke would do. But Duke was brave. Fred wasn't. If he saw a runaway dog food truck, he'd probably run the other way.

The alley was quiet. Except for the sound of Fred's paws slapping against the wet pavement.

There was a streetlamp up ahead. Its misty cone of light shone on a dumpster.

There might be food in there! Fred realized. He heard the muffled clanking of dishes. Sniffed the delicious odor of steak and meat loaf and baked potatoes. Because the dumpster was right behind a restaurant!

He picked up his pace and trotted over to inspect the hulking treasure chest. His nose wiggled and widened, savoring all the smells.

An elderly dog, so skinny Fred could see its ribs, stepped into the light and pawed at the dumpster.

Man, thought Fred, *that old guy looks even hungrier than me.*

Suddenly, a tough, muscular bulldog with a spiked collar emerged from the darkness.

The bulldog was growling.

ANOTHER MEAN-LOOKING DOG, a Doberman pinscher, slunk out of the shadows behind the bulldog.

The Doberman's collar was spiky, too.

"Whatcha doin', Grandpa?" the bulldog grumbled.

"Well," replied the old-timer, his voice shaky, "I was hoping I might find something to eat inside this dumpster. You see, I've fallen upon hard times and—"

"Boo-hoo," sneered the bulldog.

"Yeah, boo-dee-hoo-dee-hoo," snickered the Doberman.

"Step away from the buffet, Grandpa," commanded the bulldog. "This is our alley and our dumpster."

Fred was still hidden by shadows, but he crawled forward. Inching closer to the dumpster.

He wasn't sure why. He just did it.

"Come on, friends," begged the old dog. "Surely there's enough scraps inside for all of us."

"Ah, quit your whining," barked the bulldog. "My name is Dozer, see? And I ain't your friend. The only dog I'm sharing my dinner with is my pal here, Petunia."

"Do not make me rip out your fur, old man," snarled Petunia. "Because you ain't got much fur left!"

Fred had never been brave. In fact, he was pretty much a coward.

But for some reason, Dozer and Petunia reminded him of Mike and Big Tony. They were all bullies, and bullies were only interested in what they wanted, not who they might be hurting.

Fred was tempted to sneak away and hide. But he couldn't let the two mean dogs rough up a weak old stray who looked like he might not even have any teeth. So Fred rose up out of his crawl and stepped into the dim light cast by the streetlamp.

"Um, you guys?" Fred was so terrified, he wondered if the bulldog and the Doberman could hear his heart thumping inside his chest. Yep. This had been a really bad, terrible, no-good idea.

"What the what?" gasped Dozer. "It's that dog. Duke!"

"Huh?" said Fred.

"Duke!" shrieked the Doberman. "From *Dog Squad*!"

"I knew they'd nab us one day!" said Dozer.

Fred glanced down at a puddle and studied his reflection.

Okay. There was a resemblance. He didn't have the

same heroic glint in his eye, and his fur didn't ruffle as majestically in the breeze, but he did look a little like Duke. Especially in the murky light of an otherwise dark alley.

"Cheese it, Petunia!" cried Dozer.

The tough dogs took off.

Fred laughed a nervous laugh. "I'm not Duke, I'm—"

But they were long gone.

"Thank you, young fella," wheezed the old dog. "You're very brave."

"Me? Not really. I was actually kind of scared. Did you see the fangs on that Doberman?"

"I certainly did. But true courage doesn't mean you're not afraid. True courage means you're scared but you go ahead and do what needs to be done anyway."

Fred helped the old dog forage for food in the dumpster. Mission accomplished, he found a few scraps for himself, too.

It was food. Sort of. But it was also disgusting.

Suddenly, a rattling truck crunched up the alleyway.

"Uh-oh," said the old dog. "Now *we* better 'cheese it'! That's Animal Control!"

THE OLD DOG moved fast.

He darted behind the dumpster just as a man dressed in coveralls climbed out of the truck. The man carried a long pole with a loop at the end.

"Well, hey there, big guy," he said to Fred, sounding very friendly. "You lost?"

Fred wagged his white-tipped tail. He did that sometimes when he was nervous.

"I'll bet you're hungry, too."

Fred's tail swished even faster. He *was* hungry.

"How about I take you someplace nice and cozy where they'll feed you two meals a day?"

Fred's whole body was wiggling now. He did need someplace to spend the night. And he was still hungry.

"Just need to loop this around your neck . . ."

The man slipped a soft circle of rope over Fred's head. Fred smiled. This was his lucky night! This nice man was

going to take him someplace safe where he could eat two
meals a day! Maybe a restaurant. Maybe he'd get to slurp
down stringy spaghetti like he'd seen dogs do in a cartoon
once.

The man tugged on a smaller loop at his end of the
four-foot pole.

The rope cinched around Fred's throat.

"Ha! Gotcha!" the man shouted triumphantly. "You're
comin' with me, fleabag."

Fred's whole body slumped. The man had tricked him.

Big Tony was right. Fred was dumb. Now he might wind up someplace even worse than Big Tony's!

The man tugged hard on the pole and dragged Fred over to his truck. Its cargo area was a series of locked and vented doors. He opened one and shoved Fred into what turned out to be a very cramped, very dark prison cell. Fred felt the loop loosen around his neck and was about to smile in gratitude just as the jail door slammed shut in his face.

"'Someplace nice and cozy,'" the man said sarcastically. "'Two meals a day!' You dogs always fall for that one!"

Fred heard the man climb into the cab and close his door with a heavy thud.

Just when Fred had thought things couldn't get worse, they had.

His whole world jerked forward as the truck rumbled up the alleyway. Fred turned around and around, trying to get comfortable inside his very uncomfortable cage. A little light leaked in through the locked door's air vents whenever they passed underneath a streetlight. Otherwise, Fred was surrounded by darkness.

"Well, well, well," muttered a familiar voice behind him. "Look what the cat dragged in. If it ain't Duke hisself."

It was Dozer. The bulldog who'd been tormenting the old dog at the dumpster.

"Actually," said Fred, "my name is—"

"Shuddup! I only got snatched because of you. I ran the wrong way. Headed south when I shoulda gone north. Petunia? She escaped. I didn't. Because of you, Dookie. You're the reason they're hauling me off to the big house!"

"I'm very sorry if—"

"I told you to shuddup, Duke!"

"I'm not—"

"Gonna live very long? Yeah, you got that right. How much you wanna bet this doofus in the coveralls is hauling us off to a kill shelter?"

A KILL shelter? All of a sudden Fred's whole world was swirling. He felt like he was in the middle of a raging river without a raft.

"You know what that means?" said Dozer. "If you ain't adopted in two, maybe three, weeks, they're gonna give you the big needle and put you to sleep!"

Okay. Now things had gone from bad to worse to even-more-worse. The truck wasn't cold, but Fred started to shiver.

"Oh, yeah," gloated Dozer. "They're gonna kill you, Duke. Unless, of course, I kill you first!"

FRED HAD A lot of time to think, locked up in his cell at the New York City Animal Control Center.

He thought about how he'd had a big family when he was born. Three brothers and two sisters. Life was warm and cozy. But then he had to say goodbye to his littermates and his mom because it was time for Fred to be part of a new family.

With Susan!

She wrote his name on his collar and bought him a comfy bed and all sorts of toys. And food? Oh, the food was always delicious. Susan even let Fred have a pinch or two of the chicken off the top of her salad. Once, she let him have a whole hamburger. Just the meat, no bun, but the meat was all Fred wanted. Sometimes, Susan also let Fred sleep in *her* bed.

But then Mike came along and Fred ended up in a shelter. Maybe this same one.

So here he was. Right back where he'd started. Waiting for someone to give him the one thing no dog can give himself: a home.

There were dozens of other dogs yapping and barking and anxiously pacing around in their cramped cages. Cuter dogs. Smarter dogs. Much more adoptable dogs. Some were purebreds.

Fred was what somebody once called a bitzer. A little bit of this, a little bit of that. A mixed-breed mutt. Part boxer, part hound, part who knows what.

Fortunately, the tough guy, Dozer, had been placed in a different section of the shelter where they locked up the dogs who snapped at the handlers or bit the bars of their cages.

Dozer's buddy Petunia was locked up in the same section. A different Animal Control officer had snatched her off the street about an hour or so after Dozer and Fred were caught.

"You doing okay?" asked a dog Fred couldn't see.

He looked around. Wondered who might be talking to him.

"Yo. Down here, pal. Yoo-hoo."

Fred tilted his head and, in the bottom of the cage next to his, saw a miniature Chihuahua with pointy ears shaped like Doritos (something Big Tony had liked to eat for breakfast).

"Wait a second," said the Chihuahua. "You're you!"

"Huh?"

"You're that dog. From that show. You're Duke!" The little dog was spunky and very animated. "Dun-dee-dun-dun-dun! 'When trouble calls, it's Dog Squad to the rescue!'"

The little dog made Fred laugh. It was a relief to see a friendly face after so many snarly ones.

"I hate to disappoint you, but I'm not Duke. I'm just Fred. I know I sort of look like Duke. . . ."

"Are you kidding? You two could be twins. Anyway— pleased to meet you. I'm Chico."

"Pleased to meet you too, Chico."

"I can't get over it. You look just like Duke. You could be him!"

"No I couldn't. Duke is dashing. Sophisticated. And brave."

"Ah, everybody's dashing, sophisticated, and very brave on TV," said Chico. "So, you're lookin' for a new home, huh?"

"Yep. But I don't think I'll find one. I've already had two. Lost 'em both. I'm starting to think maybe I'm the problem."

Chico gave the air a good sniff. "Nah. Your breath is fine. You gotta have hope, Fred!"

"Hope?" said Fred. "They're just gonna keep me here a week or two and then put me to sleep."

Chico laughed. "They'll do what?"

"Put me to sleep. This is a kill shelter, after all."

"What? Who told you that?"

"A bulldog named Dozer."

"Dozer? From the alley? Forget anything he told you. That guy puts the *bull* in *bulldog*. You and me? We got nothin' to worry about, pal. We're finding our forever homes. Watch this."

Chico did a series of backflips.

"Wow," said Fred. He was impressed.

"Oh, yeah. Folks love the backflips and other amusing antics. What can you do, Freddy?"

Fred thought about it.

"Does wrestling a couch cushion count?"

"It's a start. What else have you got?"

Fred thought some more.

"One time, on *Dog Squad,* they had to hop over a bunch of laser beams or they'd set off a burglar alarm. I taught myself how to do it. Memorized all the moves. You should've heard Susan laugh when she saw me doing it just like Scruffy did. She gave me Snausages."

"Niiiice," said Chico. "So, show me your stuff, Freddy Boy."

"Okay." Fred rose up on his hind legs and hopped around the cage. "You just have to pretend that you're trying to escape from international diamond smugglers."

Fred and Chico danced and hopped and laughed and almost forgot about the prison bars between them. It

reminded Fred of
when he was only
a few weeks old,
horsing around and
roughhousing with
all his brothers and
sisters. He hadn't
had this much fun
in a long, long time.

The other dogs
in their cellblock
started barking.

"Hey, they're cheering us on!" said Chico.

The other dogs barked even louder.

Not because they enjoyed Fred and Chico's moves.

But because two handlers were strolling up the center
aisle between the rows of cages.

"Those two," said a woman carrying a clipboard.

She pointed at Fred and Chico.

"Definitely," said the other handler. "They both need
to go. Right now."

Fred and Chico froze.

"I thought you said this wasn't a kill shelter," Fred
whispered.

Chico gulped. "I might've been wrong."

THE LADY HANDLER gave her partner the clipboard. Then she leashed Fred and Chico and escorted them out of the kennels.

So, thought Fred, *this is it. The end of the line. I'll never find my forever home. Or my forever family.*

When they reached the lobby, they saw a man at the front counter. Fred pulled back and tried to hide behind a water cooler. His legs quivered. His pulse quickened.

"Fred?" said Chico. "What're you doing?"

"Hiding!"

"Why?"

"That man! He's the one who tossed me out into the alley."

Big Tony had his back turned to Fred as he spoke to the Animal Control Center receptionist.

"The name's Tony Bomboloni. My friends call me Big

Tony. I'm a dog whisperer. You give me your toughest cases. I'll turn them into first-class guard dogs. Find them forever homes."

Fred scooched closer to the water cooler and accidentally nudged it sideways—enough to make the big water bottle up top wobble.

"Easy, big guy," said the lady holding his leash. "We need to head outside. The van is waiting."

"The van?" screeched Chico. "They're going to put us to sleep in a van?"

The lady led Fred and Chico outside.

Fred kept his head down. He didn't want to go to the van, but he also didn't want Big Tony to see him. Yes, Fred wanted a home. But not that one. He didn't need to be told how dumb he was a dozen times a day. He'd been there, done that. Didn't want to do it again.

Sometimes when you had choices, there just weren't any good ones. Like that time the Dog Squad was stranded between a volcano and an alligator pit. Of course, Duke, Nala, and Scruffy had jetpacks, so that made their dilemma a little easier to deal with.

Fred wished he had a jetpack. But he didn't. All he had was the collar around his neck.

"Okay, guys," said the handler when they were outside on the sidewalk. "If you need to go, do it now. You're going to be in the van for fifteen or twenty minutes."

Chico looked to Fred. "Fifteen or twenty minutes?

It's gonna take them that long to put us to sleep?"

Fred shrugged. "Maybe they read to us first?"

He had no idea.

He just knew that his life, which had only been two years long, was coming to an end before it ever really got started.

"HEY, DON'T LOOK so worried," said the lady. "This could be your lucky day. You guys could end up on Broadway!"

Chico and Fred exchanged quizzical glances.

Wait—what?

Broadway?

"You two are such hams!" she said. "That dance you did? Do something like that when we get to the audition, okay? Full disclosure? I'm pretty sure it's an audition *and* a publicity stunt. A dozen dogs from animal shelters all over New York will get to try out for the two remaining dog roles in *Washington!* It's kind of like *Hamilton.* You know—a hip-hop musical. But you guys won't have to sing. You'll just be some of George Washington's dogs. Jenny Yen is the animal trainer on the show. She's a real pro. Broadway, TV, movies."

Fred looked at Chico. Chico gave him a grin.

"I told you, Freddy Boy. You gotta have hope!"

The driver kept talking. She was a real talker.

"Jenny Yen has done it all. Her niece Abby is awfully cute, too. Abby thinks she's a pet psychic. We work with Jenny and Abby all the time. They love training strays because, come on, you guys are the best, am I right?"

The lady smiled up into the rearview mirror. It was a good smile. Sincere.

These had been the weirdest few days in Fred's life, but for the first time in a long time, he relaxed.

Chico, too.

"A Broadway musical?" gushed Chico. "We could be famous, Fred. And when you're famous? Everybody wants to adopt you!"

Fred wagged his tail to that. If Chico was right, then they'd do this show, become big Broadway stars, and wind up with forever homes. Maybe Susan and Mike would even want him back if Fred all of a sudden became a famous dog. They could show him off in Central Park. *"Oh, your dog is a purebred? Well, ours is a star!"*

The lady parked the van and whisked Fred and Chico into a room with a shiny wooden floor. Ten other dogs and their handlers were already there, waiting patiently on the first row of bleachers. Fred saw a clump of TV cameras and photographers and eager reporters with notebooks.

"Wow," said Chico. "This is sooooo exciting."

"Yeah," said Fred. "We're gonna get homes."

Five people, all of whom looked like they loved what

they did, whatever it was, came into the room and sat behind a long table.

Fred had a good feeling about the woman with the shiny black hair and the swirling arm tattoos. She seemed . . . happy!

"Hi, folks," said the tattooed lady. "I'm Jenny Yen. This young lady to my left is my assistant and niece, Abby."

Fred caught Abby's eye and smiled. She winked and smiled back.

"As you all know," Jenny continued, "the cast of *Washington!* needs two more dogs."

She lowered her eyes and focused on the line of dogs gazing up at her.

"In case you guys hadn't heard, George Washington was a big dog lover. His favorite dog was named Sweet Lips."

The people all laughed. The dogs all smiled and panted. Fred swished his tail across the floor. Who knew George Washington was a dog person? No wonder America was such a great country.

"Okay, let's get started." Jenny looked down at her clipboard. "Where's Chico?"

Chico yapped. A very high-pitched yap followed by a very high-energy wiggle. Everybody laughed again.

"It's showtime, Freddy Boy!" said Chico. "Showtime!"

CHICO DASHED OUT to the center of the open floor.

Jenny Yen was holding a reward—a small meaty treat.

Chico sniffed it, and when Jenny raised her hand, he went up on his hind legs and started doing a bunny hop.

Fred had never met a dog like Chico. He had all sorts of moves and wiggles and shimmies. When Jenny raised her treat hand even higher, Chico did a backflip for his big finish.

Everybody applauded.

"He's fantastic!" said Jenny, slipping Chico the treat. "A little firecracker!"

"I agree," said a very serious-looking man with one of those beards that Fred thought made people look like schnauzers. "But he's too small."

Chico's eyes bugged out. He looked worried.

No, no, no, thought Fred. *Chico is perfect.*

But Fred knew being perfect wasn't enough when you were a dog. Sometimes people just didn't like the way you looked. Or the color of your coat. Or your pedigree.

To make things worse, Fred heard Chico whimper. It was a sad, pitiful, almost musical whine.

"Excuse me?" said one of the photographers, a man who'd snapped about a bazillion pictures during Chico's dance routine. "Is Chico available for adoption?"

"Yes!" Everybody at the table answered at the same time.

"Excellent," said the photographer. "Chico? You're coming home with me!"

The room erupted with applause.

"Oh, yeah," said Chico. "That's what I'm talkin' about. Life is good! Keep the faith, Fred!"

Fred had a lump in his throat the size of a meatball. He'd only known Chico for a few hours. But the little guy felt like his best friend in the whole world!

Ten other dogs auditioned. Including a female chow chow named Cha-Cha from a purebred rescue group.

Fred had to wait. And wait.

The chow chow sidled up beside him.

"What, exactly, are you supposed to be?" she asked.

"Excuse me?" said Fred.

"What's your breed?"

"Oh. I'm what they call a bitzer. A little bit of this, a little bit of that."

Cha-Cha elevated her snout a little higher. "I see. No wonder you don't have an absolutely fabulous fur coat like mine. I suppose we purebreds have all the luck."

"Yeah," said Fred. "I suppose you do."

FINALLY, JENNY LOOKED down at her clipboard and called for Fred.

"Good luck," sneered Cha-Cha. "You're going to need it."

This was it. His one chance. Maybe his last chance. None of the other photographers looked like they were in the mood to adopt a dog today. Besides, Chico was tiny. He could fit inside a camera bag. Fred weighed sixty-five pounds and—

"Fred?" This time Abby was calling for him. "You're up."

Fred took a deep breath and scampered out to the center of the floor.

"Hey, Aunt Jenny!" said Abby. "Check it out. Fred looks just like Duke!"

"Huh. You're right. But don't worry—I won't hold it against him. All right, Fred. Sit."

Fred sat.

"Down." Jenny lowered her flat, outstretched hand, so Fred went flat on his belly. "Good boy!"

Fred said "Thanks" with a thumping tail wag.

"Look at his smile!" said Abby. "And those eyebrows!"

"They're wonderful. And . . . up!"

Fred hopped up on his hind legs and did a little of his hopping-over-laser-beams dance. People were laughing. And clapping. Some were even whistling.

"Good boy!" said Jenny, feeding him a small treat as a reward. "You're amazing!"

When she said that, Fred had no choice. He had to jump up into her arms and give her a smooch.

It was a good thing Jenny Yen was strong, because Fred was pretty heavy. She caught him and cradled him. Fred dragged his tongue across her face—all the way up to her eyebrows.

"Okay, okay," Jenny giggled, gently lowering Fred to the floor. "You've got the part. You're going to be in the show!"

Abby gave him another wink and two thumbs up.

Fred couldn't remember when he'd ever been this happy.

This felt good.

This felt like home.

FRED AND CHA-CHA, the second audition winner, rode with Jenny and Abby to an apartment in Brooklyn that the *Washington!* producers had rented for their canine cast.

"We're going from the cage to the stage," said Cha-Cha. "See what I did there? That rhymed. Cage. Stage. I'm extremely talented, aren't I?"

Fred smiled. It was the polite thing to do.

Jenny piloted her specially outfitted dog transport van into a neighborhood filled with cozy brownstone town houses. The kind where families lived. Some were even out walking with their dogs!

"By the way," said Cha-Cha, "did you know that I'm a purebred chow chow?"

"Yes," said Fred. "You told me."

"We're famous for our magnificent coats."

"You told me that, too."

"Did I mention my purple tongue?"

Cha-Cha stuck out her tongue at Fred. It really was purple.

"Okay," said Fred. "That is awesome!"

"I know. I should be on TV. This Broadway musical? Just a stepping-stone. Jenny Yen trains dogs for all sorts of shows, including my fave, *Dog Squad*."

Fred gasped. "*Dog Squad*? She knows Duke, Nala, and Scruffy?"

"Uh, yeah," said Cha-Cha. "She trains them. Oh, and by the way: I don't care what the giggly little girl says."

"Her niece?"

"Yeah. Gabby."

"Her name is Abby."

"Whatever. You, my friend, are no Duke."

Fred and Cha-Cha didn't talk much after that.

When Abby led Fred into the Brooklyn brownstone, he was astonished.

Wow! he thought. *This isn't just a home, it's a magical palace!*

The dogs had two whole floors, connected by a steep staircase that Fred couldn't wait to race up and down. There was a big room with a fireplace, which would be, as Nala always said, "pawsome" in the winter. (All the *Dog Squad* holiday specials had roaring fires in them, and Scruffy usually dragged in the biggest log.) There was a chef in the kitchen making special dog meals. A dog chef! It had to be the nicest home Fred had ever seen. Even nicer than Susan's place. At Big Tony's and the animal shelter, Fred had slept on the floor. Here, Abby showed him his own fleecy dog bed, and it was heated!

Fortunately, all the other dogs in the show, the ones already living in the town house, seemed friendly. Maybe because all of them used to be strays and were grateful for their second chances.

Fred particularly liked Ethel, a sharp-tongued shih tzu.

"She better be careful," Ethel said when Cha-Cha strutted into place to pose for a "Dogs of *Washington!*" publicity photo the next day. "If that chow chow flicks her fluffy fur one more time, I swear it's going to fly off."

Fred couldn't believe all the tall, shiny buildings when they drove into midtown Manhattan for their first rehearsal. It reminded him of the *Dog Squad* episode where they all used hang gliders to soar from skyscraper to skyscraper until they cornered the bad guy on the observation deck at the top of the Empire State Building.

At the theater, Ethel helped Fred learn all the steps for the big "Mount Vernon" number after Jenny went over and over them with all the dogs.

Fred wasn't a natural dancer like Chico, but no dog in the cast worked harder than he did. It was like Nala always said on *Dog Squad*: "Hard work beats talent if talent doesn't work hard!"

Jenny noticed.

"Fred is fantastic," she said to Abby.

"And he's a good dancer, too!" Abby said with a laugh.

"Let's move him up to the front of the chorus line with Ethel."

During a rehearsal break, Abby hugged Fred.

"You really are fantastic!" she said. Then she whispered something odd in his ear. "I'm a pet psychic, Fred."

"No she's no-ot," singsonged Ethel.

"I can hear your thoughts."

"No she canno-ot," said Ethel.

"Go on, Fred," said Abby. "Think something."

Fred was thinking about peeing. They'd been rehearsing for three hours straight and he'd really been hitting the water bowls hard, so he needed to head outside. Soon.

"I've got it!" Abby said excitedly. "You want to go outside and smell the flowers!"

Actually, he wanted to go outside and *water* the flowers, but she was close enough.

"Wow," said Ethel sarcastically. "I guess even a broken clock is right twice a day."

THE DOGS AND humans rehearsed for three full weeks.

Every Thursday night, Fred and the other dogs from the show would hang out in the living room of the Brooklyn brownstone and watch *Dog Squad* together.

Fred's favorite episode was the one where Duke, Nala, and Scruffy had to ski off a cliff in Switzerland to chase down the villain, who had stolen a top-secret chocolate formula.

"We're just trying to make the world a little sweeter," Duke said after the Dog Squad rolled the bad guy down the slope and turned him into a giant snowball.

"Even though dogs should never eat chocolate," said Nala.

"I guess chocolate's the one thing that's too ruff for us!" joked Scruffy.

Then all three dogs tossed back their heads and laughed

at the Alps. Duke had the most heroic-looking laugh. Especially with his ski goggles propped up over his eyes just so.

"I'm going to star on that show some day," bragged Cha-Cha as the end credits rolled.

"Ha!" sniped Ethel. "In your dreams. No, wait. Not your dreams, *my* nightmares!"

All the other dogs, including Fred, laughed at that. Cha-Cha didn't have the right stuff for *Dog Squad*. All she ever seemed to think about was herself. Heroes always thought of others first.

The next day, they were back at rehearsal. BOOM! The drummer was banging his biggest kettledrum to make it sound like a rumbling cannon. As much fun as doing the show was, Fred wasn't a big fan of the music in *Washington!* It was kind of loud, and loud stuff made Fred jumpy. Thunder? Worst. Noise. Ever.

A very talented actor played the lead character, Gee DoubleYou. Everybody said he had "good flow."

But the lyrics? Ethel, who'd been in a bunch of Broadway shows, said they were terrible. Especially the big opening number:

> *Please look me in the eye,*
> *Because I cannot tell a lie.*
> *The one who cut the tree?*
> *To tell the truth, that was me.*

"This show might belong next to a bowl of mashed potatoes come Thanksgiving," Ethel snarked. "Because it sure smells like a turkey!"

Even if the show was bad, Fred had a great time at rehearsals. Since school was out for the summer, Abby was with Jenny all the time. During breaks, she'd try to read Fred's mind. She'd also talk to him. A lot.

"You're a really nice dog, Fred," she said, sitting down on the floor beside him. "You're very easy to talk to. I think dogs are easier to talk to than people, how about you?" Abby laughed when she realized what she'd just said. "Anyhow, there's this boy. Zachary Babkow. He's my age. Lives up the road from our ranch. His dad, Mr. Babkow, is our new handyman. Anyway, Zachary comes by sometimes to help his dad, and he seems really nice and stuff, but I wish I could talk to him the way I can talk to you."

Fred placed his head in Abby's lap. She stroked his ears.

Fred hoped that one day, he'd be able to help Abby. It was what families did. They helped each other.

FINALLY, IT WAS time for opening night!

Backstage at the theater, everybody was buzzing with excitement. Fred was nervous. Maybe more nervous than anybody, even the guy playing Gee DoubleYou.

He remembered what Chico had said. Dogs who were stars automatically found homes. He peeked out at the audience from behind the big velvet curtain. There were a couple of definite possibilities out there. Families who looked like they might need a dog. Others looked more cat-ish. But still, he had hope!

To calm himself, Fred needed a breath of fresh air, so he made his way over to the stage door, where Johnny, the security guard who checked folks in, sometimes kept the door propped open on hot nights. Johnny wasn't at his post. Fred figured he was off getting a cup of coffee.

But then Fred heard sobbing.

Outside. In the alley that led from West Forty-Fourth Street to the theater's stage door.

Fred poked his head out to see who was making the noise.

It was a young boy, about six, in a *Lion King* T-shirt and shorts. Tears were streaming down his cheeks.

He's in trouble, thought Fred, hearing his favorite theme music in his head. *And when trouble calls . . . it's Dog Squad to the rescue!*

Fred knew he needed to be onstage. Soon. But he remembered what it felt like whenever he was alone and afraid.

He scurried out the door and trotted over to the boy.

"I'm lost!" the boy wailed. "Daddy?!"

Fred tried to reassure the boy with a happy tail wag.

It didn't work. Now the boy was crying uncontrollably.

Fred had to find the boy's parents.

He barked once to let the boy know he'd be back, then dashed up the empty passageway to the street.

West Forty-Fourth Street was crowded. Throngs of people were jockeying for position in ticket lines that snaked up and down the block.

How could Fred ever find the boy's people?

What would Duke do?

No—what would Nala do!

She'd lock in her laser-sharp eyes and focus, focus,

focus. "Don't see the herd," Nala had famously said in the *Dog Squad* "Dude Ranch" episode. "See the cows."

Fred needed to see the cows. The ones who had lost their calf.

He saw a man buying a hot dog at a cart. It looked delicious. There was a couple taking a selfie in front of a big *Washington!* poster.

There!

A man and a woman. Ten yards away. They were clearly panicking. Looking left, looking right. Flailing their arms. Talking to other people. All of them shrugging.

Fred barked and raced up the crowded sidewalk.

He planted himself right in front of the rattled parents.

He wouldn't stop barking.

At first, the man and woman were just annoyed and pressed past Fred to ask other people if they'd "seen a boy, six years old, in a *Lion King* T-shirt?" Fred followed them. He kept barking.

Finally, the woman gave Fred a dirty look. But it softened quickly. She turned to the man. "Do you think . . . ?"

"Impossible," said the man. "He's just a dumb dog. Probably a stray."

Fred barked louder and jerked his head to the left.

"Follow me!" he said, and jogged a few paces toward the alley.

The people didn't follow him.

So he said it even louder. "FOLLOW. ME!"

Finally, the woman understood. Fred led the way and she followed him. The man threw up his arms and decided to follow too.

Fred took them into the stage door alley.

"Ethan!" they both shouted as they raced to their son and hugged him.

Fred smiled. Families were best when they were together.

The man turned to Fred.

"I'm sorry I called you a dumb dog," he said.

Fred gave him a tail wag to say, "No hard feelings, sir." He thought about adding, "Saving puppies is what we do best," but the man wouldn't understand.

"Hey, Mom," said the boy, wiping his nose clean with the back of his arm. "That's one of the dogs. From *Washington!* I saw his picture out front!"

"We're coming to see you tonight!" gushed the boy's mother.

Oops. Fred needed to be onstage when the curtain rose for the first act. He didn't want to disappoint Jenny. He didn't want to miss his chance to find his forever family, who might just be waiting for him out in the audience.

The parents escorted their son back up the alley. They were both holding his hands this time. Fred grinned.

Mission accomplished, he thought. Feeling great, he scampered toward the stage door.

Cha-Cha was on the other side of it, smirking.

"Sorry," she said. "By order of the fire department, this door must remain closed at all times."

She nudged it with her snout.

And the heavy metal thing slammed shut.

Fred was locked out.

THE SHOW STARTED without Fred.

Fortunately, Johnny, the security guard, opened the stage door at intermission.

"Hey, buddy, where were you?" said Jenny, rubbing Fred's head.

"We were so worried!" said Abby.

Fred's heart sank. He'd missed his chance.

The audience and the critics LOVED the dogs, who only appeared in the first act of *Washington!* Unfortunately, they hated everything else.

Fred never made his big Broadway debut.

Washington! closed after one performance.

The brownstone in Brooklyn would not become Fred's forever home. And nobody in the audience was going to adopt him because nobody had ever even seen him.

THE NEXT MORNING, Fred took one last lap around the apartment.

It'd been nice while it lasted.

Some of the dogs would be staying in their warm and cozy beds. Jenny would work them into other shows.

Ethel would be returning to the cast of her last show, *Put On Your Shoes.*

"Now in its fifth smash year," she proudly proclaimed.

"Thank you for all your help," Fred told her.

"My pleasure, Fred. I've never known any dog with more heart than you. So what's next?"

Fred shrugged. "I don't know. Maybe they'll send me back to the shelter."

"What? No way. Once Jenny Yen rescues you, you stay rescued."

"Really?"

"Really. As long as she can afford to keep her Second Chance Ranch running, you'll always have a home."

A wave of relief washed over Fred.

"Pawsome!"

"Careful," Ethel joked. "That's Nala's catchphrase."

"Right. My bad. I have to go thank Jenny!"

Fred bounded down the staircase and padded into the kitchen.

Jenny was on her phone. She didn't look happy.

"Duke broke his leg?" she said to whomever she was talking to. "How bad is the fracture?"

Abby was sitting on a stool. She looked miserable too. But when she saw Fred, her eyes lit up like she was having an idea. Or maybe she'd just seen the box of doughnuts on the counter near the sink. Fred couldn't tell.

"How long will it take for the leg to heal?" Jenny asked. "Two weeks?! We have a big grand opening at Pet World tomorrow. They booked Duke to cut the ribbon."

"Aunt Jenny?" said Abby.

"Hang on, hon," said Jenny, covering the phone with her hand. "Duke did something stupid. He'll be in a cast for two weeks."

Jenny's phone thrummed. She looked at the screen.

"Dr. Appleman?" she said to the phone. "I'm going to have to call you back. The *Dog Squad* people are beeping in." She poked the screen. "Hey . . ."

Fred heard a man screaming through the speaker. It

was hard to understand. But Fred could tell: the man was not happy.

"Yes," said Jenny, "I know it's a grand opening. But we need to postpone."

"No we don't," said Abby.

Jenny covered the phone again. "Abby, honey? This is serious."

"Duke can still do the Pet World promotion tomorrow."

"Can you hang on for just one sec?" Jenny said to the phone. "I need to, uh, take this other call."

Jenny pressed Mute.

"Abby? Duke is injured. Dr. Appleman says he can barely hobble out of his doghouse."

"So it's a good thing we have Fred." Abby was so excited, she sprang off her stool and bounced up on the balls of her feet. "Fred looks enough like Duke to fill in for him. He's even got the lightning bolt of white fur on his head."

Jenny didn't say a word.

She looked at Abby.

She looked at Fred.

She looked back at Abby.

Abby nodded. "It'll work, Aunt Jenny. I know it will."

Finally, after a really deep breath, Jenny unmuted her phone.

"Sorry to keep you waiting," she said. "Don't cancel the pet store event. We're good to go!"

15

"YOU'RE COMING WITH us," Abby told Fred. "The Second Chance Ranch is awesome! You'll see."

Fred was about to climb into Jenny's special van for the trip to Connecticut, a place he'd never been before. In fact, Fred had never been outside New York City in his life!

"You've ended up in the gravy, my friend," Ethel told him. "The gray-vee! The Second Chance Ranch has ninety-two acres. There's a barn and doghouses that are, hello, houses for dogs. You'll probably share a room in one of the bigger kennels with a bunch of others. When I'm up there, I, of course, have my own private bungalow. So does Duke. Nala and Scruffy share a cute cottage."

Fred was amazed. "All three of them are really there?"

"Yep. The biggest dog stars in the world live at Jenny's place."

"Wow!" Fred couldn't believe his good luck. He was going to live in the same place where his heroes lived.

"You'll meet 'em all. Duke, Nala, Scruffy, Reginald . . ."

"Who's Reginald?"

"Golden retriever. Stars in all those TV commercials for the minivans and the fancy shampoo? He does the YourHouse Real Estate and Taco Bob spots, too."

"That's a real dog? The one who knows how to make tacos?"

"Yep."

"Come on, Fred," called Abby.

She patted her hands on her thighs.

Fred turned to his friend. "So long, Ethel!"

Ethel gave him a happy yap, and Fred scrambled up a ramp into the back of the van.

"You're next, Cha-Cha." Abby turned to the chow.

Ugh. Cha-Cha's coming, too? Oh, well.

Fred was too happy to let her ruin his day.

"I hope I get a bigger crate this time," grumbled Cha-Cha, sashaying up the ramp as if she was in a fashion show. "The last one was so tiny the bars crimped my fur like a waffle iron."

Fred settled into his crate. Jenny started up the van. Abby clicked her seat belt. They were on their way.

"We were great last night," Cha-Cha said with a self-satisfied sigh to no one in particular. She was, once again, in the crate right next to Fred's. "Those of us who actually made it onstage, that is."

Fred tuned her out and enjoyed the ride north to

Connecticut. He'd never seen so much green. And rolling hills. And beautiful blue skies filled with puffy white clouds. And when Abby powered down the windows? He'd never smelled such fresh air or so many trees and flowers.

It reminded him of the secret location of the Dog Squad Command Center. Before every mission, Duke, Nala, and Scruffy raced across a meadow filled with wildflowers to a stump. After making sure no spies were watching, Duke would slap his paw on the stump because it had a secret wooden button. Once Duke bopped the button, the whole hillside would open up, like a grassy, hinged dome, and reveal the triple entrance slides down to their high-tech subterranean lair. The three heroes hopped into their individually labeled tubes and slid down to their briefing stations, where they were surrounded by blinking computers and glowing video screens.

Every episode, they'd listen to their assignment, always delivered by Top Dog himself—a five-star, 130-pound bullmastiff military commander who worked for some very important humans in Washington, DC—and then plot their preparations.

"If we fail to prepare," Duke would remind his teammates, "then we are preparing to fail!"

Nala would bark, "Pawsome!"

Scruffy would declare, "Nothin's too ruff for us."

And then, boom—they'd be off on another adventure.

Fred sighed contentedly. He knew he'd never have that

kind of adventure, but it sure sounded like he might get to romp through a grassy meadow!

TWO HOURS LATER, when the van finally pulled into the Second Chance Ranch, Fred could actually smell the nearby ocean. It was salty with a hint of fish.

"Welcome home, Fred!" said Abby as he leapt out of the van.

Yep.

She'd said it again.

This was Home!

ABBY OPENED THE door on Fred's crate.

"Go on, Fred. Have fun!"

Fred flew down the ramp and tore across the open field, just like they did on *Dog Squad* and in all those dog food commercials. After about thirty minutes of pure joy, romping in the grass and chasing butterflies, he heard Abby whistle for him.

"Come on, boy. It's time for you to meet your twin. It's time to meet Duke!"

Fred's heart skipped a beat.

He was going to meet Duke? THE Duke?

The dog who'd saved the Queen of England's corgis?

The dog who had his own submarine?

The dog who'd blasted off in a rocket ship and saved the crew of the International Space Station?

Yeah. That was the dog Fred was about to meet. That was why his legs were quivering again. It was hard to walk with quivering legs, but Fred followed Abby as best he could.

"So here's the plan, Fred," said Abby. "Tomorrow, you're going to *be* Duke."

As if that was remotely possible! Fred thought.

Duke was the dog of dogs. The king of the canines. No one could ever even pretend to be half as heroic as Duke was.

"Relax," said Abby, picking up on Fred's anxiety. "It'll be easy. Go inside. Spend a little time with Duke. Get to know Nala and Scruffy, too. They're in there, visiting."

Fred did his best to wag his tail cheerfully.

On the one paw, the idea of pretending to be Duke, the most courageous dog on television, terrified him.

On the other, knowing he was about to meet his favorite action heroes—Duke, Nala, and Scruffy—also terrified him.

He cautiously crept up to the porch and—after pausing to take in a deep, fortifying, leg-steadying breath—shimmied through Duke's doggy door.

"Hey, look, Duke!" said the wiry terrier Fred immediately recognized as Scruffy. "It's you."

Scruffy, of course, was the scrappy, funny one with the New York accent. Fred smiled, remembering the time Scruffy saved a cat stuck in a toilet bowl and then accidentally flushed himself into a swirly whirly.

Nala was right next to Scruffy!

Fred LOVED Nala. She was so wise. So athletic. If

dogs were ever in the Olympics, Nala would be the captain of every dog team. Who could ever forget her amazingly gymnastic tumble through zero gravity on her space walk in that episode about the space station?

"It's like we're looking in a mirror," she said, shooting Fred a wink.

Duke himself was sitting in a very cushy, very regal dog bed—his right front leg wrapped in a plaster cast.

Fred could not believe where his life had taken him.

This was the moment he'd been waiting for.

He was in the presence of Duke.

He was about to express his gratitude for all Duke had done and meant. All the lessons he had taught.

But Duke spoke first.

"If you were looking in a mirror," Duke snapped at Nala, "you'd see yourself, not me. And why'd you bring me flowers?" he grumbled to Scruffy.

"We figured you needed something to smell," said Scruffy. "What with you being cooped up inside and all."

"You figured wrong, dumbbell. You know what happens to dumbbell sidekicks?"

"No, Duke," said Scruffy. "What?"

"They get *kicked* to the *side*. You're both replaceable. Remember that."

"Oh, I will, boss," said Scruffy. "I will. Gonna make a mental note . . ."

While Scruffy babbled, Nala gave Fred a look. An eye roll.

Suddenly, Duke, the hero Fred had admired his whole life, turned his full attention to Fred. His eyes were cold.

Fred was in shock.

Because so far, the real-life Duke was nothing like the noble and heroic one Fred knew from TV.

In fact, the two Dukes couldn't've been more different!

17

"SO," SAID DUKE with a dismissive snicker, "I hear Jenny Yen thinks you look like me."

Fred nodded and gave an awkward smile.

"I don't see the resemblance," said Duke. "You're a stray, straight from the shelter. Me? I'm the most heroic dog in the world!"

Fred was stunned speechless.

"Can you speak?" asked Duke.

Fred didn't know what to do. So he barked.

"Ha!" laughed Duke. "The fool barked. Like when humans say, 'Speak!' Now, *that's* comedy. Funnier than anything you've ever done, Scruffy."

Scruffy's whiskers twitched. Fred could tell: that insult stung. Nala moved closer to Scruffy and struck a protective pose.

"Listen up, you mutts," snarled Duke. "Jenny's dumb idea of having this nobody doubling for me is only temporary. Fine. He can pretend to be me at the pet store opening. I don't care about pet store openings. I don't really do pet store openings anymore."

"We did that one last week," mumbled Scruffy.

"Scruffy? When I want your opinion, I'll give it to you."

Duke returned his focus to Fred. "Listen and listen good, whatever your name is."

"Um, it's Fred, sir."

"So? I don't need to know your name because we're never going to converse again. Got it?"

Fred's body and spirit drooped. This was not how he'd pictured this conversation going. Not at all.

"Yes, sir." He whispered it.

"Tomorrow, at the pet store, you don't bark, you don't shake paws, and you definitely don't do any of my signature moves. You just stand there looking like me for a few minutes and tear down the ribbon when Jenny tells you to. Is that clear?"

"Yes, sir."

"Now, scram. All of you. I'm healing here. And take your lousy flowers with you!"

Scruffy snatched the limp flowers off the floor.

"Come on, kid," said Nala, gently nudging Fred toward the door with her snout.

Fred felt like he might burst into tears. Duke had been his hero. His idol. On TV, anyway. In real life? He was closer to Big Tony.

When they were about ten feet away from Duke's front porch, Scruffy spat out the flowers he was carrying in his mouth. "Paaaaa!"

Then he lowered his voice and gave Fred a little advice. "Don't let Duke get under your fur, kid."

"He's rude and nasty to everyone," added Nala. "He doesn't get easier. We just have to get stronger."

"But he's Duke," said Fred. "He's the most heroic dog in the world."

"Yep," said Scruffy. "And he's also the most obnoxious dog in the world."

EARLY THE NEXT morning, Abby came to the kennel
Fred shared with a dozen other dogs.

Fred had the worst bed in the room. Cha-Cha had
made him sleep in a corner.

"You snore!" she claimed.

Fred didn't really mind sleeping in the corner. It was as
far away from Cha-Cha as he could get.

"How you feeling, big guy?" Abby asked, scratching
Fred behind his ears.

Oooh. Fred was feeling particularly good right then
because Abby had just hit the magical spot that made his
right rear leg jiggle.

But then he thought about what he was about to do:
stand in for Duke. Pretend to *be* Duke. No way could he
pull that off. And what if the real Duke heard how badly
he'd done? He was definitely in over his head.

"Aw, that's so sweet," said Abby after squinting hard

at Fred for maybe a minute. "Remember, Fred: I'm a pet psychic, so I'm picking up your thoughts!"

"What's he thinking?" asked Jenny, coming into the kennel with a leash.

"That he won't let this go to his head," said Abby.

Ohhh-kay, thought Fred. She was close. Sort of.

Jenny took off Fred's old collar and replaced it with one Fred recognized from TV.

It was Duke's!

"This is just for today," said Abby. "And don't worry. Your collar will still be here when we get back."

Jenny hooked on a leash and led Fred outside to where Scruffy and Nala were waiting. Abby followed them.

"Hiya, Fred," said Scruffy. "How'd you sleep last night?"

"Not so good," said Fred.

"Because you were thinking about Duke, am I right?"

"Yeah."

Nala sighed. "What consumes your mind, Fred, controls your life."

Scruffy nudged his head toward Nala. "She spent some time at a goat yoga spa. Picked up all sorts of wisdom. Tell him that one about—"

"Duke?" said a very noble-looking golden retriever, prancing over to join the group. "Why on earth are you sleeping in a kennel filled with background dogs, old bean? Have you been demoted?"

"Um, I'm not really Duke. I'm Fred. Duke's double."

"Really? My, what an uncanny resemblance. I'm Reginald Farnsworth of Collingwood the Fourth. I'm a purebred. A true golden."

"And a true prima donna," sniped Scruffy out of the side of his snout.

"Wait a second," said Fred. "You're the star of all those TV commercials. You can make tacos! And drive an SUV! You even know how to save everybody fifteen percent on their car insurance."

"Yes," said Reginald. "Word of advice, Fred? Never work with lizards. They're snakes."

"Are you coming with us?"

"Indeed I am," said Reginald. "Duty calls, and all that tommyrot."

"Okay, you guys," said Jenny, clapping her hands together. "Into the van. It's a half-hour drive to the pet store."

Abby hooked a leash on Reginald's collar. "We're gonna have fun!"

"Oh, I'm certain we will," said Reginald sarcastically. "Who doesn't love a good pet store opening? Especially if they have balloons."

"IT'S DUKE!" SHRIEKED a young fan. "From *Dog Squad*!"

Suddenly, three hundred people, including lots of kids, started screaming, clapping, and cheering. The family dogs they'd brought along for the pet store's grand opening barked and yapped and howled.

Fred had just stepped out of the van (wearing Duke's famous collar) and was walking down a red carpet behind Nala and Scruffy.

Nala turned around to give Fred some words of encouragement. "Keep calm and bark on."

That bucked him up. Nala was like a coach. She knew what to say to help others be their best.

The three dogs made their way through the throng of people and pets, past bunches of balloons and flapping banners. They marched toward the entrance of a huge superstore, where two columns of stacked dog food sacks rose like lumpy towers.

"It's that other dog!" Fred heard a young girl shout. "The one who makes tacos every Tuesday!"

Fred glanced over his shoulder. Reginald had stepped out of the van. Abby held his leash.

As Reginald realized the size of the crowd, his eyes widened in what looked like fear. Or panic. Maybe both.

"This way," said Jenny. She led Fred, Nala, and Scruffy to a thick yellow ribbon that was tied on either end to the two food bag towers. Fred sniffed the air. So did Nala and Scruffy.

"Peanut butter?" said Nala.

Scruffy nodded. "Pure Jif. Chunky style."

"I love peanut butter," said Fred, licking his chops.

"Then today's your lucky day," said Scruffy. "Just wait for Jenny to give us our cue."

"Anticipation of pleasure is a pleasure in itself," Nala remarked wisely.

"Sit," Jenny commanded.

The three dogs sat, waiting for Reginald to complete his walk down the red carpet. But he seemed reluctant to come any closer. Abby tugged on his leash.

Reginald dug in his paws and refused to budge.

"There are too many people!" he fumed.

"This is Reggie's first public appearance," Scruffy whispered to Fred.

"He's used to cameras, not crowds," added Nala.

"Up, Reginald!" said Jenny.

The crowd oohed and pitter-patted their hands. They couldn't wait to see what Reginald might do.

But Reginald just stood there.

Doing nothing.

20

REGINALD'S LEGS SHUDDERED. His lips curled back in queasy distress. He looked like he was about to puke.

The crowd grew restless.

"Make a taco!" someone jeered.

"Save me fifteen percent on my car insurance!" shouted someone else. "Open up the door to the home of my dreams!"

"Ms. Yen?" said a man in a Pet World polo shirt. "Our contract specifically stated there would be dog tricks."

"Reginald is just a little nervous," Jenny explained.

"Well, what about Duke?"

Jenny turned to Fred. So did Abby. Her brown eyes seemed wider than dog bowls. Fred wasn't a psychic, but he knew what his new young friend was thinking.

Fred needed to put on a show. He remembered what Chico had said about people enjoying amusing antics. Hey, Jenny and Abby had given him a home. The least Fred could do was give this crowd a little entertainment.

He leapt up on his hindquarters and launched into the routine Chico had taught him at the animal shelter. Then he added some of the moves Ethel had shown him for *Washington!*

Scruffy and Nala joined in, following Fred's lead.

The crowd loved it. They were cheering and clapping and shouting, "Go, Duke! Go, Duke!"

"Way to save the day, 'Duke'!" said Scruffy, who'd added a funny butt wiggle to his dance moves.

"Nothin's too ruff for us!" said Nala.

"Hey," said Scruffy. "That's my catchphrase!"

The two friends laughed. Fred laughed with them. Wow. He actually felt like he was part of the Dog Squad! *But,* he told himself, *this is only temporary. This is just for today. Tomorrow you go back to being just Fred.*

Then he remembered Nala's famous line from the *Dog Squad* holiday spectacular where the trio saved Santa from the angry polar bear: "Today is my tomorrow!"

So, Fred decided, today was his day to have fun and enjoy being Duke!

Jenny hauled Reginald back to the van.

Fred and Nala kept dancing while Scruffy hopped over to the yellow ribbon.

"Go for it!" Abby shouted.

"Ennn-joy!" Fred and Nala told Scruffy. They wanted to keep busting a move.

Eager for peanut butter, Scruffy leapt up, bit into the ribbon, and yanked it down hard.

Maybe too hard.

Because the ribbon had been strung too close to the

mounds of dog food. Tugging the ribbon jostled the pillars on either end.

The stacks started teetering.

Fred looked up. The pile on the right was about to topple over.

And crush the baby stroller parked right beside it!

FRED'S INSTINCTS KICKED in immediately.

He barked and bolted for the baby carriage.

Behind him, he heard Nala shout, "Dog Squad to the rescue!"

Fred raced toward the right tower, leapt into the air, and slammed his front paws into the stroller. His impact sent the baby buggy rolling backward. The baby's mother screamed and went chasing after her child.

The crowd pointed up at the swaying column of fifty-pound food bags.

"Get out of the way!" shouted a man.

"It's coming down!" cried a woman.

There were screams. Shrieks. Panic. But everybody got out of the way seconds before all those heavy bags crashed to the pavement.

Fred looked to his left. Nala and

Scruffy (well, mostly Nala) had safely herded their side of the crowd out of harm's way too. Someone came up behind Fred and wrapped their arms around his neck.

"Thank you, Duke!" sobbed the mother. "You saved my baby. You're a hero, Duke! A real hero!"

Fred wagged his tail. He probably should've told the lady that he wasn't really Duke and he definitely wasn't a hero, but she was giving the top of his head so many kisses it was hard to get a word in edgewise.

Abby ran over.

"Are you okay?" she asked.

"Yes," Fred said with a panting smile. Now that the scary stuff was done and nobody had gotten hurt, he was fine, just fine.

Jenny soon joined them. And Nala and Scruffy were with her.

"You have the right stuff, Fred," said Nala.

"And not just on the dance floor, kid," said Scruffy. "You gotta teach me how to do that leap-push-shove thing. I could use that in the show."

Jenny bent down and looked Fred in the eye. "Thank you" was all she said. And then she said it again. "Thank you."

Fred felt warm and fuzzy inside. It was good to be able to give something back to the family that was already giving him so much.

The man in the polo shirt came over.

"Thank you, Ms. Yen. Thank you, Dog Squad."

He gestured toward the toppled bags of dog food. Several had split open. There was a sea of spilled kibble bits spreading across the asphalt parking lot.

"If your dogs are hungry," said the Pet World manager, "looks like we're giving away free samples."

Jenny laughed. "Thanks. But we'd better get these guys home."

Abby gave Fred another head rub. "They're pooped. Being heroic is exhausting work."

"DID YOU GUYS see that?" said Scruffy for the fifth time on the way back to Jenny's place. "Trouble called, and Fred raced to the rescue. He leapt up, and BOOM! He pushed that baby buggy to safety."

"It reminded me of the circus episode," said Nala. "Where Duke saved the daring young man on the flying trapeze."

"Maybe," said Scruffy. "But Fred here was working without a net."

"I underestimated you, Frederick," said Reginald.

"I was just, you know, following my instincts," Fred said modestly.

Reginald shook his head. "Don't sell yourself short. You not only saved that toddler, you also saved me. I must admit, I was suddenly, and shockingly, frozen in fear."

"Fear has two meanings," said Nala. "Forget Everything And Run. Or Face Everything And Rise. The choice is yours."

Reginald gave her a look. "Exactly how much time did you spend with those goat yoga people?"

Soon the van's tires crunched into the pebbly driveway at Jenny's place. Her cell phone, docked on the dashboard, started chirping.

"Can you put that on speaker, hon?" she said to Abby.

Abby tapped the screen.

"Hello?" said Jenny.

"Jenny? It's Leo."

"Leo Espinosa is the creator of our show," Scruffy informed Fred. "Nice guy. Wears too much cologne. Know what I'm saying?"

Fred just nodded.

"We need to ramp up the schedule," he heard Leo say. "We're hearing rumors of fresh competition. A new show called *Seal Team Seven*. With real seals. We need new episodes. We have to start shooting in two days or they could crush us."

"Two days?!" said Jenny.

"Is that a problem?"

Scruffy and Nala turned to Fred.

Abby whirled around in the passenger seat.

Jenny looked up in the rearview mirror.

They were all smiling expectantly at Fred.

"Leo?" said Jenny. "Can you give me a second?"

She tapped the Mute button on the phone.

"What do you think, Fred?" she asked. "Are you ready for the big leagues?"

"You were exceptionally awesome today," added Abby.

This was it.

Fred gulped. The idea of playing Duke a little longer was terrifying.

But maybe it was time to do like Nala said.

To Face Everything And Rise.

"Yes!" Fred barked. "Yes, yes, YES!"

"FRED?" SAID JENNY. "Come with me. I want you to spend a little more time with Duke."

Ohhh-kay, thought Fred. *Not my first choice.* The truth was, their first visit had been more than disappointing. It had been downright disillusioning. If Fred couldn't believe in his hero, who could he believe in?

"Can I come too, Aunt Jenny?" asked Abby.

"Sure."

"Today was a good day to have a good day, Fred," said Nala. "Thank you for that."

"Let's skedaddle, guys," said Scruffy. "It's dinnertime up at the bungalow."

Nala, Scruffy, and Reginald bopped up the hill to the doghouse the three stars shared.

Scruffy was sniffing the breeze. "I think they're serving meat. Oh, yeah. I'm smellin' steak! T-bone, baby!"

"See you guys later," Fred called out to his new friends.

Sure, Duke had been a major disappointment. But Nala and Scruffy? They were even more amazing in person.

Fred held his head high and practically floated alongside Jenny and Abby. It felt good to have done good. To have made some new friends. To be told he'd been "exceptionally awesome."

"Hiya, Abby!" a voice called from up near the road. It was a very nice-looking boy, about the same age as Abby, helping a man roll out some green mesh fencing. The boy looked like he got a lot of fresh air and exercise.

Abby held up her hand just high enough to wave a weak hello.

"Hiya, Zachary," called Jenny in her big, booming voice. "How's it going, Mr. Babkow?"

"Just fine," said the man, who Fred now figured was the boy's father.

Fred remembered Abby telling him about Zachary.

"Need to patch up a few spots over behind the barn next," called Mr. Babkow, fastening the fencing to its post.

"Thanks, Jim!" said Jenny.

"Let me know about starting work on that new kennel."

Jenny laughed a little. "I will. Right after the bank lets me know if I can afford to do it."

Now Mr. Babkow laughed. "Oh, I know how that goes."

"See you round, Abby!" called his son.

Abby gave Zachary another half wave and mumbled, "See you round."

Oh, yeah. She definitely needed major help in the dialogue department.

When they crossed the field and reached Duke's doghouse, Jenny turned to Fred.

"Go on inside," she said. "Spend some time with Duke. Soak up whatever you can."

"The good stuff," added Abby. "How he acts in the TV show, not real life."

"Right," said Jenny. "No need to imitate *that*."

Fred put on a brave face and scampered up to Duke's floppy pet door.

"Um, knock, knock, sir."

There was no answer.

"Knock, knock, knock?"

Still no reply. So Fred eased his way into the doghouse.

Duke, wearing a sleep mask, was sprawled out in his dog bed. His chin was propped on the plaster cast covering his front right leg. He also wasn't paying any attention to Fred's arrival.

"Uh, hello? Hate to disturb you, sir."

"What? Who is it?" grumbled Duke.

"It's me, sir. Fred. Your stand-in?"

Duke slowly peeled up one flap of his sleep mask with his good front paw.

"You ever sleep on a plaster pillow?" He worked his

head around in circles. "Very uncomfortable. So how was the thing at the thing?"

"Oh, the pet store opening?" said Fred excitedly. "Extraordinarily awesome, sir."

Duke pulled off the sleep mask. "Yeesh. You sound like Abby."

"I guess I do. . . ."

"Well, cut it out. I find her to be extraordinarily annoying. All that pet psychic garbage. If she can communicate with animals, how come she can't hear me telling her to knock it off?"

"I don't—"

"That was a rhetorical question—meaning I'm not really interested in hearing an answer from you."

"Oh. Okay . . ."

"So, why are you here, waking me up? Were you expecting me to say, 'Good boy. Thanks for filling in for me at the ribbon-chomping ceremony'?"

"Oh, no, sir," said Fred. "I never thought you'd do that."

"You thought correctly."

"It's just that Jenny thinks I should study you some."

"Study me?"

"Your facial expressions and gestures."

"What? Why?"

"Because, well, it's only for a little while, until, you know, you get better. . . ."

"What are you blubbering about?"

Fred blurted it out. "Jenny wants me to fill in for you on *Dog Squad*."

Duke's eyes went wide. His snout spasmed. His top lip curled back and exposed a pair of angry incisors.

"You're kidding. Right?"

Terrified, Fred shook his head. "No, sir."

"YOU CAN'T 'FILL in' for me!" growled Duke. "Nobody can fill in for me. I'm Duke. Without me, *Dog Squad* isn't worth watching."

"Well, sir," said Fred earnestly, "I watch every episode, and Nala is amazing and Scruffy is funny. I definitely think *they're* both worth watching."

"Only because you're an idiot. Why on earth would Jenny Yen even consider replacing me with . . . *you?*"

"Because they need to start shooting new episodes right away. Now, I've been working on arching just one eyebrow like you do when—"

"Don't you dare! Jenny can wait. They can all wait. My cast will be off in two weeks."

"But they need to start shooting in two days. It sounds like an emergency."

"Emergency? It'll be a disaster."

"Well, like I said, it's only temporary. Now, could you show me how to do some of your other heroic poses?"

"Not. Going. To. Happen. I will not take part in this charade. I am the one and only Duke. You are a fraud. A phony! And a fake!"

Okay. That went even worse than Fred had feared.

"Get your ugly snout outta my house! And don't come back!"

Fred skittered out of the doghouse with his tail tucked between his legs.

How many houses am I going to get thrown out of?

Abby was waiting outside with a big smile on her face. So Fred put one on his, too.

"Come on," said Abby. "Aunt Jenny wants you to help pick your new costar. The next script has a puppy in it!"

Fred's ears perked up.

A puppy?

That might be exactly what Fred needed to forget about Duke!

WILFORD, CONNECTICUT, HOME to the Coastal Animal Shelter, was only a five-minute ride from Jenny's place.

"That's where we found Scruffy," Jenny reminded Abby.

Abby had decided to ride to Wilford in the folded-up back seat right next to Fred's crate.

"That's the beach, right across the street, Fred," she said. "Over there? That's the Scoop Sloop, where we get ice cream sometimes. I'll get you some vanilla yogurt next time we go."

"You and Zachary could bike there," suggested Jenny.

"I guess," said Abby, sounding shy again. "Oh! That cheesy motel right next to the animal shelter is called the Seaside Sandman."

Fred smiled. The excited bubbles were back in Abby's voice.

"In history class, we learned that the Wilford Grand Hotel used to stand in that exact same spot, only it was totally trashed in 1938 by a storm everybody called the Big Wind. My teacher, Mrs. Meckley, says the storm surge was so high, it ripped the Wilford bridge right off its moorings!"

"Mrs. Meckley does a good job."

"She's better than good, Aunt Jenny. She's pawsome."

"Ha. You sound like Nala."

Jenny pulled the van into a slanted parking spot in front of a very modern-looking building with giant silhouettes of a dog and cat flanking a heart on its tallest wall.

"Come on," Jenny said, checking the notes in her folder. "Let's go meet our potential puppy, Tater Tot."

They climbed out of the van.

"We're supposed to call Fred 'Duke,' right?" said Abby as she clipped on his leash.

Jenny nodded. "I don't want anybody to know we're working with a stand-in. Duke will be back on the job in less than two weeks."

"My lips are sealed." Abby rubbed Fred's head. "You ready to go inside and meet Tater Tot . . . *Duke*?"

Fred barked once to answer in the affirmative.

The instant he stepped down into the parking lot, though, he started working his nose and sniffing at the breeze.

Jenny took in a deep breath too.

"I love the smell of the ocean."

"And it's right over there, Duke," said Abby. "Right across Atlantic Avenue."

Fred had never been this close to the shore before. When he really listened, he could hear waves crashing. He had a sudden urge to dash across the street so he could romp in the foamy water like Scruffy did in the *Dog Squad* episode where the team, decked out in full scuba gear, landed on the beach in a rubber raft. Scruffy kicked off his flippers so he could slap the sand with his "bare paws."

"It's squishy!" was a catchphrase that people and dogs repeated for months after hearing Scruffy say it first.

Of course, Duke reminded Scruffy that they were on a mission, not a vacation. The beach was on an island where an evil mad scientist was developing a laser

beam that could blast satellites out of the sky. The Dog Squad was there to pull the plug and "neutralize his ray gun—before the madman ruins satellite TV for everyone. It's football season!"

Still, Fred *would* like to romp in the surf the way Scruffy did in that episode.

Someday. But today Fred had a job to do. He needed to be Duke and go meet a puppy named Tater Tot.

"HI, JENNY," SAID a lady in a white coat standing
behind the animal shelter's reception desk.

"Hi!" Jenny looked down at Fred. "Duke? This is Barbara Wolin. Be nice to her. She's one of our best talent
scouts."

Ms. Wolin laughed. Fred could tell that she and Jenny
were pals.

The lobby was extremely hot. Its floor-to-ceiling windows coupled with the bright summer sun were turning
the place into a greenhouse. Fred panted. He wasn't an
orchid.

Abby started fanning herself.

"Sorry," said Ms. Wolin. "Our air conditioner decided to take its vacation in the middle of August, just
like everybody else."

"That's okay, Barbara," said Jenny. "From that photo
you texted me, I'd say Tater Tot is worth it."

"Definitely. Come on. He's out back in the dog run, where it's nice and shady. Oh, by the way—every single one of the puppies you used in the river raft scene found a forever home. Rocko, of course, went first."

"That's what I love to hear!" said Jenny. "Every animal deserves a second chance. Now let's go meet Tater."

Fred followed the humans out the back door and into a narrow fenced-in patch of dirt and scrubby grass. It was long but not very wide. A dog could have a blast running back and forth inside it.

"Tater?" called Ms. Wolin. She put her hands on her hips and scowled. "Stop that, Tater! Now! No dig."

Fred had to smile. The beagle puppy was a scamp and a digger.

Tater was attempt-ing to burrow a tunnel underneath the fence. He stopped the instant Ms. Wolin commanded him to.

He whipped around to say he was sorry and froze. He'd just seen Fred.

"Wowzers! You're you! Duke. From TV. I'm your biggest fan."

While Tater gushed, all the humans heard was a frantic series of high-pitched yaps.

"He's adorable," said Jenny. "We can't wait to work with him."

"What're we gonna work on, Duke?" Tater asked with wide-eyed wonder when he heard Jenny say that. "Are we gonna build somethin'? I'm buildin' an escape tunnel like you guys did when that bad guy trapped you in that dungeon!"

Fred realized he'd never had to sound like Duke when talking to another dog before. At Pet World, he hadn't said anything to any dogs except the ones from Jenny's place, who knew who he really was. Now he'd have to imitate the Duke he knew from TV (not the snarky one he knew from the doghouse).

First he chuckled a macho chuckle. Then he cocked up a single eyebrow.

Awestruck, Tater just sighed.

"Hey, Tater," said Fred. "How'd *you* like to be on TV?"

"With you?"

"Yep. Plus Nala and Scruffy, of course."

"They're amazing. But you're even more amazing. You're Duke!"

"Tater is perfect!" proclaimed Abby. "And he looks great next to Duke."

"Then it's settled," said Jenny. "Tater is our star puppy for episode three-point-six, 'Undercover Cat-Tastrophe.'"

"Is there a cat in it?" asked Ms. Wolin.

"Yep," said Jenny.

"Come on. Let's go inside. We'll fill out the paperwork

for Tater Tot. Then I can show you guys a few cats. They all need good homes too."

Jenny turned to Fred and Tater. "Behave while we're gone. We'll be right back."

Fred sat.

Tater sat too.

But as soon as the three humans were gone, he scurried back to the fence to finish digging his escape tunnel.

"There's something sweet and salty on the other side of this fence, Duke!" Tater yipped.

"I think you're just smelling the ocean, little buddy."

"I'm almost out!" Tater scooched under the fence.

All Fred could see was his wagging tail.

And then—POP!—Tater was gone.

"WOO-HOO!" TATER SHOUTED as he scampered through the landscaped lawn behind the animal shelter. "Come on, Duke! Let's go see the ocean!"

The puppy leapt over a concrete curb and onto the driveway circling the building. He was out of sight in a flash.

The ocean is on the other side of that busy street! Fred realized. *On the other side of all that dangerous traffic! And Tater is barreling right into it!*

Think, he told himself. *What would Duke do?*

The answer was easy: TV Duke would chase after Tater and rescue him.

But there was no way the sixty-five-pound Fred could squeeze through the puppy's narrow escape tunnel. Maybe he should go alert Jenny.

No. There wasn't time. Horns were already honking out on the busy boulevard.

Fred would have to go *over* the fence, not under it. He'd have to clear the hurdle like he'd seen the Olympic-caliber leaper Nala do in the *Dog Squad* episode where she cleared an electrified fence in a single bound.

Fred hurried to the far end of the narrow strip and ran! As fast as he could. As his snout was about to smack into the wall, he sprang up, pushed off the ground, and soared like a furry rocket over the pointy tips of the stockade fence.

He hit the ground on the other side, still running.

He did it!

He couldn't believe he'd done it, but he had!

He whipped around the corner of the building. He could see Tater, toddling across the busy street.

"Excuse me!" the puppy peeped. "'Scuse me."

Cars and trucks slammed on their brakes. A motor-cycle swerved. Tires squealed. More horns blared.

Tater wobbled and wove his way through heavy traffic and, finally, reached the other side of Atlantic Avenue. The ocean side.

That meant Fred had to cross the busy street too.

It's what Duke would do!

Fred darted into traffic. Tires screeched. A truck blasted its air horn. Angry drivers leaned out of car windows to shake their fists.

One man hollered, "Watch where you're going, you dumb . . ."

But then he quit screaming.

"Hey! You're Duke. That dog from TV!"

Fred stopped in the middle of the street and smiled. The driver held up his phone and snapped a quick selfie.

"Love your show, man!"

Fred barked to say a quick "Thanks" and resumed his zigzagging scramble across the sizzling asphalt.

Woof. That was extremely dangerous. But he made it to the beach side.

Tater, though, had disappeared.

FRED SNIFFED THE breeze.

There were a lot of aromas wafting in the wind. Salt. Water. Sand. Sandwich. Something with sausage. Onions and green peppers, too.

Focus! he told himself.

Another sniff and he picked up Tater's scent.

Fred let his nose take the lead. He spied Tater down on the beach, frolicking where the sand was gray and wet. He was thwacking his paws in the muck, chasing the sudsy waves. When the curling surf raced back to the shore, Tater let it chase him up the beach.

"Tater!" Fred called.

"Hey, Duke!" Tater called back. His tail swung so happily it was a blur. "Woo-hoo! The ocean is playing chase with me!"

"We need to go back!" Fred insisted as he strode across the sand.

"In a second, Duke. Look. There's something jiggly in the water. It's like a flat rubber pull toy made out of clear gunk! It even has all sorts of strings to play with."

"No, Tater!" Fred roared.

He knew in a flash what Tater had just found. Because Fred also watched a ton of nature shows on the Discovery Channel.

It was a jellyfish. Probably a lion's mane because it had so many "strings," which weren't really strings or hairs or a tangled lion's mane but lots and lots of tentacles.

The sticky kind with stingers!

"GET OUT OF the water!" Fred barked at Tater.

"B-b-but—"

"It's a jellyfish!"

Fred didn't have time to think, only to act.

Another blast of instinct and adrenaline fueled Fred's next move.

Churning up sand, he raced to where the curious puppy was poised to paw at the jellyfish.

Fred flew through the air and splash-landed in the shallow water, putting himself between Tater and the stinging lump of jiggly jelly junk.

Fred wiggled and whooshed his whole body back and forth, churning up a whirlpool of murky salt water.

Yes!

Just like the Discovery Channel said it might, his body shuffling stirred up the water so much it terrified the jellyfish. The slimy thing oozed out to sea, dragging its tentacles behind it.

No one got stung.

Not on my watch! thought Fred, hearing TV Duke's voice in his head.

Fred stood up and gave himself a good shake. Water droplets splattered Tater in the face. But the surprise saltwater shower didn't stop the puppy from gawping up at Fred in awe.

"Wow!" said Tater. "Did you just save my life?"

Fred was panting hard. "I don't know. Maybe. What I do know is that those stingers would've really hurt you, Tater. Jellyfish are poisonous."

"You did! You saved my life, Duke! Just like you do on *Dog Squad*. Only, this wasn't TV. This was real. With

real poison. I could've gotten really sick."

Tater gasped. His shoulders slumped. His tail stopped flapping. He gave Fred his saddest puppy-dog-eyes expression.

"I'm sorry, Duke."

"It's okay to make mistakes, Tater. As long as you learn from them. Did you learn something today, little buddy?"

"You bet I did. If you're going to do something super dangerous, make sure Duke is right there with you!"

Fred laughed. Laughing came easy when he was pretending to be Duke. Even being brave seemed easier.

"This has to stay our secret," he told Tater.

"Oh, I won't tell anybody. I promise. Cross my heart and hope to dribble drool."

"Good. Now, come on. We need to head back."

"Sure, Duke. Whatever you say, Duke. You know best, Duke."

Fred's smile grew a little wider.

It felt good to be Duke. Really, really good.

FRED AND TATER were back inside the dog run when Jenny, Abby, and Ms. Wolin came to get them.

(Tater crawled under the fence; Fred executed another Nala-style high jump.)

"It's official," announced Ms. Wolin, picking Tater up for a goodbye snuggle. "You're going to be on *Dog Squad*!"

"And after the episode airs," added Jenny, "I guarantee you'll find a forever home."

Ms. Wolin passed Tater to Jenny.

"His paws are kind of damp," she said. "I think he hasn't learned how to lift his leg when he . . . you know."

Jenny laughed. "He's a puppy. He'll learn."

Fred wagged his tail. He hoped Tater learned some other stuff too. Like not to run across busy streets or splash around with jellyfish.

THE NEXT MORNING, Jenny and Abby loaded Fred, Nala, and Scruffy into their crates for their van ride to "the set."

Dog Squad would be shooting most of its next episode on location at someplace called the Four Paws Spa, a "Luxury Pet Pampering Boutique." It was about two hours away, over in Millville, New York.

In the script, the spa was the front for a sinister criminal mastermind who was spying on very important people by planting listening devices on their pets. Dr. Ludlow Loofah was the bad guy, selling top-secret information to the highest bidder.

"You're going to do some absolutely amazing stuff, Fred!" Abby said as she flipped through the script in the passenger seat. "It's so cool!"

The cat from the animal shelter, Clarence, would be in the first day's scenes too. Tater would arrive on set and shoot the day after that.

"I love when we go on location!" said Scruffy as the van rumbled west. "We get to stay in a hotel with the crew. A lot of them order beefy burgers from room service!"

Fred raised both eyebrows. Confused.

"When they finish their dinners," explained Nala, "they leave their trays on the floor outside their door, where a hotel staff person is supposed to pick them up and take them back to the kitchen."

"But until that happens," said Scruffy, smacking his lips at the memory, "that food is fair game, baby. It's good and easy hunting, which, by the way, is my favorite kind of hunting. Word to the wise? Stay away from the pickles."

"I choose not to eat table scraps," said Nala. "I need to stay in tip-top condition at all times."

"I don't," laughed Scruffy. "I'm the funny sidekick, not the agile and athletic one."

The cast and crew of *Dog Squad* rented two entire floors in a Millville hotel near the Four Paws Spa location. Fred had never realized how big a team Duke needed to be, well, Duke.

Fred, Scruffy, and Nala shared a room. It had a door connecting them to Jenny and Abby's. Jenny had set up "wee-wee" pads in the dogs' bathroom.

"We never use them," Nala told Fred. "It's a matter of pride."

"We wait for a walk," added Scruffy. "We aren't animals."

"Hey, you guys?" asked Fred. "How come those cups up on the sink in the bathroom are wrapped in plastic?"

"To keep them sanitary," said Nala.

"Yeah," cracked Scruffy. "This may be a pet-friendly hotel, but they sure don't want us licking the insides of their cups!"

Room service waiters brought the three dogs their dinner, and like the rest of Fred's wonderful new world, it was absolutely unbelievable. There was steak on his plate! Steak! Sure it was something the hotel called Salisbury steak, but it was awesome. And it came with brown, lumpy gravy! Fred could definitely get used to this.

After dinner, Scruffy went to the full-length mirror and wiggled his face and whiskers.

"What're you doing?" Fred asked, genuinely interested.

"Working on my facial expressions," said Scruffy. "Watch this."

He flapped up his ears and bugged open his eyes.

"I look surprised, right?"

"You do!" said Fred. "You totally do. Let me try."

Fred made funny faces at the mirror.

"Draw on your past experiences," instructed Nala. "Remembering a surprise will bring surprise to your face."

Fred thought about the time Susan had made him a meat loaf cake with mashed potato frosting for his birthday. Now, that was a surprise!

In the mirror, Fred's face lit up with genuine amazement.

"You learn quickly, grasshopper," said Nala with a wink.

"That's a neat trick," said Fred. "Let's do more!"

"Knock yourself out, guys," said Scruffy with a yawn. "That big dinner made me snoozelly. I'm hitting the hay. Five a.m. comes awfully early."

"Five a.m.?" said Fred.

"Yep. That's when we head to the set. Starring in a TV show isn't all glitz and glamour. Okay, it's mostly glitz and glamour, but you also have to wake up early."

THE NEXT MORNING, Fred was awake before Nala or Scruffy.

He was too excited to sleep. This could be the best or worst day of his life. He was going to pretend to be Duke in front of a lot of people who knew the old Duke—the cast, the crew, the producers, the director—all of whom would think Fred WAS Duke!

If it went well, Fred would have his new "show family."

If it went poorly?

Fred didn't want to even think about that.

A little after 5:00 a.m., when the sky was just turning a pinkish blue, Jenny and Abby loaded up the three dogs and headed off to the set.

"Why do we always start so early?" said Scruffy, stretching into a yawn.

"The early bird gets the worm," said Nala.

"We're not birds," said Scruffy, slumping down in his crate. "And even if we were, no way would I ever eat worms. Not without ketchup, anyhow."

"They just want to have as much daylight as possible," said Nala. "For the camera."

Fred nodded. Scruffy snored. He could nap like a cat. Anywhere and all the time.

Speaking of cats . . .

Fred sniffed the air. Nala did too.

"What?" said a bored voice from inside a hard plastic carrier sitting on the floor between Jenny's and Abby's seats.

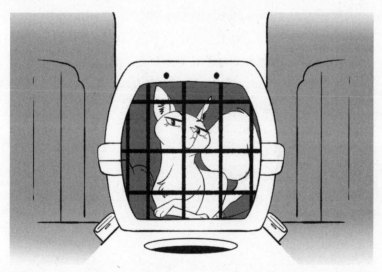

"You've never smelled a cat before?" asked the un-expected passenger. "I do it all the time. Usually their butts. You can learn a lot about a cat by sniffing its butt. You want to sniff mine?"

"Um, no thanks," said Fred.

"You're Duke, am I right?"

Fred nodded. He had to keep playing the part. "And this is Nala. She's a very courageous shepherd."

"Fear is a reaction," said Nala. "Courage is a decision."

"Whatever. I'm Clarence. I don't watch *Dog Squad*. I'm waiting for *Cat Crew*. Now *that* would be must-see TV. . . ."

"Are you going to play the Japanese prime minister's cat?" asked Fred.

"Yeah. I get in some kind of trouble at the spa. Maybe they put cucumbers on my eyes. I hate vegetables."

"Well," said Nala, heroically, "when trouble calls . . ."

Scruffy's eyes popped open so he could proclaim, "It's Dog Squad to the rescue!"

"Right," yawned Clarence. "Whatever."

"I'm glad Jenny rescued *you* from the shelter," said Fred. "You and Tater Tot, too."

"You have a tattoo?"

"No. I didn't say—"

The cat held up its paw. "Save it, Duke. I need another nap."

IT TOOK JENNY and Abby four hours to teach the dogs all their moves.

Then it was time for hair and makeup.

Scruffy wasn't happy about the stylist's plans for him.

"A bow? I have to wear a bow in my hair?"

"It's your disguise," Fred reminded him. "It's how we sneak into the Four Paws Spa. The door person thinks you're a customer."

"When they open the door to let you in," said Nala, "Duke and I bust in behind you."

"But a bow?" said Scruffy. "Come on. It's too cutesy-pootsy."

Nala put her paw on Scruffy's shoulder. "Take one for the team, Scruffy."

Fred put his paw on Scruffy's other shoulder. "Please? It's my first day pretending to be Duke in front of the cameras."

"Fine. No problem. I'll wear the bow. But I'm not watching this episode! Ever!"

"C'mon, guys," said Abby. "They're ready for you."

Fred's heart started to beat faster.

This was it!

EPISODE 3.6
"UNDERCOVER CAT-TASTROPHE"
SCENE 7

SCRUFFY, A CHECKERED blue bow bobbing in
his fur, prances up to the Four Paws Spa's
arched grand entryway, where the Japanese
prime minister's cat is secretly being held
hostage by the evil Dr. Loofah. The building
is all pink stucco and even pinker stone.
Very posh. Very pricey.

Scruffy taps the low, dogs-only doorbell
with his nose.

A slot in the door slides sideways. Scruffy
only sees a pair of eyes. Shifty eyes.

"May we help you?" asks the lady behind
the door.

"Good afternoon, ma'am. I was in earlier? You guys gave me a bow after my bath?" Scruffy gestures to it. "I think I left my collar in the waiting room."

The door opens.

Suddenly, Scruffy spins around. "Dog Squad? To the rescue!"

Duke and Nala bolt out of the bushes where they've been hiding.

The lady shrieks and runs away.

Duke leads the charge into the pet spa.

He leaps over a sunken tub, where a collie is soaking in a bubble bath. He scoots under a rolling table where a poodle's curls

are being trimmed. He passes dogs wrapped
in towels getting facials and massages.
Some have cucumbers on their eyes. Nala and
Scruffy are racing right behind him.

They aim for a door at the rear of the
spa.

A swinging door.

"That's Dr. Ludlow Loofah's evil lair!"
cries Duke.

"We have to rescue the Japanese prime
minister's cat!" shouts Nala.

"Before the nefarious Dr. Loofah puts the
microchip in his back!" barks Scruffy.

Duke knows the microchip is really a listening device. Spy gear that can eavesdrop
on all the prime minister's top-secret communications and then uplink the
classified information to
a satellite, which Dr.
Loofah will download and
sell to the highest
bidder.

Duke bursts through
the door.

Dr. Loofah looks
startled. He's wear-
ing goggles, a gown,
and rubber gloves. In

his hand, he holds a plastic microchipping gun. It's pointed at the cat's back.

"What the—?" he says, sounding shocked. "You're the Dog Squad!"

"Indeed we are," replies Duke. "Put down your surgical instruments, Dr. Loofah. Nobody's getting their back bugged today. Not on our watch."

Dr. Loofah scoops the cat off the stainless steel operating table.

"Ha!" he laughs. "Ha, ha, ha! You'll never stop me, Dog Squad! I'm far too clever for your tiny, insignificant dog brains!"

Dr. Loofah darts for a door labeled SECRET EXIT. He has the howling cat cradled against his chest.

"Don't you fools dare follow me! For I not only have the Japanese prime minister's cat. I have his new American puppy, too!"

He races out the exit and heads to . . . his waiting helicopter!

"AND . . . CUT!" CALLED the director, a tall woman with a bundle of dreadlocks. "Great job, Duke. You're really on your game today. Okay, people, that's a wrap. Tomorrow we're back here to finish the helicopter bit with the cat and puppy. Fantastic day, Jenny. Give your dogs some extra treats. Getting this much work done usually takes three days!"

"Guess they're in a hurry to head back to the hotel and check out tonight's episode," joked Jenny.

Fred realized she was right. It was Thursday. A new episode of *Dog Squad* would drop at eight. He was going to get to stream his favorite show with two of its biggest stars.

Did it get any better than that?

No, it did not.

"It's the last one we shot with the original Duke," Scruffy explained on the ride back to the hotel. "We help the president of the United States find a very important leather briefcase he lost. He needs it to stop a war."

"Duke sniffs it out," added Nala. "Right before, well, I'm not sure what. But I think it would've been a global disaster."

Scruffy nodded. "The people-actors kept telling us stuff like 'We need to move fast, Dog Squad. We have a ticking time bomb!' My heart was racing. More than usual. I'm a very high-strung individual."

That night, the three dog actors gathered around the TV set in their hotel room with a big bowl of Pork Chomps. Jenny and Abby were in their room watching the show. Their big bowl had popcorn in it.

Meanwhile, far away from the hotel, in the basement of a New York City apartment building, two other dogs were also watching TV.

Dozer and Petunia.

The snarling dogs Fred had scared away from the old-timer in the alley had both been "rescued" by Big Tony. He was training the new recruits to become guard dogs.

"Dozer," said Petunia, "I don't think Big Tony knows what he's doing."

"He's a clown," grumbled Dozer. "We're never gonna be no guard dogs."

"All he does is yell. The man has a mean streak. He's rougher on us than we ever were on all those dogs trying to mooch food out of our dumpster."

"Ha!" chuckled Dozer. "Remember that one toothless old geezer? We had him quaking in his collar."

"Yeah," said Petunia. "Good times. But then Duke came along and spoiled all our fun."

She gestured toward the TV screen, where Duke was sniffing the rear of the president of the United States' pants, trying to pick up his scent so he could track down a missing briefcase, which, according to the show, had secret codes in it.

"This show is so ridiculous," griped Dozer. "How does the president of the United States lose his top-secret briefcase?"

"And how is Duke going to find it?" wondered Petunia aloud. "There's gotta be a million leather briefcases in the world. They all smell the same. Like leather!"

"It's TV," said Dozer. "It's supposed to be ridiculous.

Ooh, ooh. Action sequence! I'm hoping this time, just for once, the bad guys teach Dookie a lesson!"

"It'd serve him right for what he did to us in that alley!" shouted Petunia.

Soon both dogs were barking and snapping at the TV set. They couldn't lunge far enough to attack the screen because they were wearing spiked collars attached to heavy chains. It hurt if they yanked too hard.

"What's all this barking about?"

Big Tony stomped down the wooden steps into the cellar.

"How'd you turn on my TV? Did one of you step on my remote? I used to have another dumb dog who did that. Kicked him out. You two want to end up like him? If not, shut up!"

He raised his balled-up fist. The dogs winced and quit barking.

"That's better."

Big Tony peered at the screen. Hard. A dog named Duke was making all sorts of heroic moves.

"Huh. The dog I kicked out looked a lot like that dog." He laughed. "They could've been identical twins except for one thing. This dog looks brave. My Fred? He was a coward!"

THE NEXT MORNING on the set, Abby had Tater cradled in her arms.

Mr. Babkow, the ranch handyman, had driven him over from Connecticut.

"Hiya, Duke!" Tater squiggled out of Abby's grip and leapt to the ground. "Mr. Babkow drove me over here really, really early. Oh, oh. Are you really Nala? Oh, oh! You're Scruffy!"

"Guys," said Fred, "meet Tater. He's here for the helicopter scene."

"Hey," said Nala.

"Howdy," added Scruffy.

"Wow! You're both you! You two are super awesome. But Duke? He's the best. He's my hero. He saved me—"

"—a Pork Chomp from last night," Fred said quickly.

He didn't want Tater to start blabbing about the jellyfish incident on the beach. If, somehow, Jenny found out that Fred and Tater had disobeyed her direct commands that day, she might kick them both off the show. Fred could lose his new home and his new family. Tater, too.

"Is Tater good to go?" asked Jenny, coming over. Fred could tell that the side flaps of her shorts were stuffed with treats.

"All set, Aunt Jenny."

"Great. Come on, Tater Tot. Let's go be cute in front of a camera."

EPISODE 3.6
"UNDERCOVER CAT-TASTROPHE"
SCENE 8

THE DIABOLICAL DR. Ludlow Loofah dashes out of the Four Paws Spa's top-secret rear exit, heading for a hornet-shaped helicopter parked in his private parking space.

He tucks the Japanese prime minister's cat under one arm like a football as he fumbles in his pockets for . . . a remote!

He points it at the whirlybird and clicks.

. The chopper's rotors start whirring, then spinning.

A very cute puppy, trapped in the back seat, presses his nose and paws up against the helicopter's smoky glass windows.

The puppy whimpers. He looks worried.

Duke, Nala, and Scruffy hurtle out the secret exit, hot on Dr. Loofah's heels.

But just as they are about to reach the copter, BAM! They slam into an invisible wall and topple backward.

"He activated some kind of force field," says Duke.

"I hate when they do that," says Scruffy.

Nala tries one more time. She lowers her shoulder and smashes into . . . something. "It's no use! We can't muscle our way through it."

"You guys?" shouts Scruffy. "The evil Dr. Loofah is climbing into the helicopter! He has the prime minister's cat and puppy!"

Duke looks left. He looks right. He looks down. And then . . . he looks up!

"There. That pole. The one with the force-field generator on top."

Nala nods. "I see it."

"It's only six feet high! That means the force field is only six feet tall. Nala? Can we clear it?"

"Not me," says Scruffy. "My legs are too stubby to jump over anything taller than a fire hydrant."

"Help!" peeps the puppy trapped in the helicopter. "Help!"

"Hurry, you two!" says Scruffy. "The evil doctor is going to get away!"

"Not on my watch," declares Duke. "Dog Squad?"

"To the rescue!" shouts Nala.

She and Duke back up so they can take a running start.

They spring off the ground and fly over the force field, setting an outdoor high jump record for dogs, just as Dr. Loofah's helicopter begins to lift off.

The scrappy puppy in the back seat, however, hops into the pilot's lap and starts gnawing on the control stick!

"That's not a chew toy, you teething little brat!" Dr. Loofah shouts over the thumping blades roaring outside the cockpit bubble.

But the puppy won't let go. He is, as they say, like a dog with a bone.

The helicopter rises off the ground.

It descends.

It goes up ten feet.

It comes back down six.

"Stop, dog!" screams Dr. Loofah. "You're making me airsick!"

The puppy sees something that makes his mouth go wide with wonder. Duke and Nala are clearing some sort of invisible hurdle like champion high jumpers.

"Yippee! It's the Dog Squad!" he shouts.

But by letting go of the control stick to shout, the puppy has returned full command of the craft to Dr. Loofah.

"Mwah-hah-ha!" the evil doctor chortles, pulling on the stick.

The helicopter rises.

"Help!" screams the puppy. "Help!"

Nala leaps into the air.

She bites down on the chopper's skids and locks her jaws.

Duke jumps next. He grabs hold of Nala's tail and scampers up her body as if it's a rescue ladder.

In no time, Duke clambers up into the cockpit and knocks out Dr. Loofah with a solid head-butt.

"Curse you, Dog Squad," the evil villain moans, slumping sideways. The helicopter tilts dangerously and almost twirls into a spin. Duke grabs the stick and regains control of the aircraft.

"Good thing I took those flight lessons on the internet," he remarks coolly.

"Nothing's too ruff for us!" shouts Nala from her perch on the left skid.

"Hey!" snaps Scruffy from over near the force-field generator, "that's my line!"

Scruffy yanks an electrical cord out of its socket. There is a warbling WOOP-WOOP sound as the invisible force field disintegrates.

Duke safely lands the chopper in the parking lot and shuts down its engines.

"Now then," he says with a cocked eyebrow. "Who wants to go inside and eat a few of those cucumbers we passed?"

Nala laughs. Scruffy laughs.

The puppy licks Duke all over his face.

The cat wakes up. "What? I was taking a nap. Did I miss something? What's this about cucumbers?"

All the dogs toss back their heads and laugh even louder.

"AAAAAAND CUT!" CRIED the director, springing out of her chair. "We got it! In one take! Unbelievable!"

"Wow," Scruffy whispered to Fred. "You're good, kid. At this rate, who needs that other Duke?"

"Jenny?" said the director. "I don't know what you're feeding Duke these days, but keep it up. He nailed every scene on the first take."

Jenny just smiled and said, "Thanks." Then she gave Fred a quick wink.

"Tater was great too," said Abby. "I'm picking up strong vibes that he'd love to be a series regular."

"Oh, I would, I would," said Tater. "If I was a regular, then I would get to see Duke on a regular basis and he's my hero because he's so brave and courageous on a regular basis."

Fred, Nala, and Scruffy stayed two more nights in

the hotel. They spent their days shooting action-packed scenes. Fred even got to pretend he was driving a very fast car with squealing tires.

It was fun. (Not as much fun as piloting a helicopter, but still.)

In between shooting scenes, Abby would sometimes take Fred for a walk.

"You're so easy to talk to, Fred. And I can tell you're really listening. Aunt Jenny's the same way. She'll listen to me blab my head off—anytime, anywhere. Unless, of course, we're on set in the middle of a scene. You can't talk after they shout 'Quiet on the set!' That would be rude."

Fred's smile widened. He liked listening to Abby.

"I wish it was this easy to talk to kids I don't really know. How do you do that? How do you strike up a conversation with a total stranger? Say something like 'Nice weather we're having'? Ha! If I said that, they'd think I was some kind of weather wonk. I'm always worried I'm going to say the wrong thing."

Fred could relate. With Big Tony, he always worried he'd *do* the wrong thing.

At night, Fred, Nala, and Scruffy feasted on Salisbury

steak, laughed about the day's bloopers, and swapped stories.

"How'd you end up at the Coastal Animal Shelter?" Fred asked Scruffy on their second night in the hotel.

"I was rescued out of a puppy mill," said Scruffy. "I was one of the lucky ones."

"Jenny found me at a shelter too," said Nala. "I remember my fur was a matted mess. I was totally out of shape. Hadn't herded anything for weeks. But Jenny saw my potential."

"I guess she saw mine, too," said Fred.

"Are you kidding?" said Nala. "We all saw it."

"That day at the pet store opening?" said Scruffy. "You saved lives, pal. Human and canine."

The next day at dusk, when shooting was finally finished, the three dogs piled into the van for the two-hour drive home to Jenny's place.

"This was so much fun," said Fred, savoring his time as Duke.

"Guess what, you guys?" said Abby from the front seat. "We just heard from Mr. Espinosa. We need to shoot some new scenes. Right away."

"There's a big push for fresh episodes," Jenny explained from behind the wheel. "The producers are terrified of that new show *Seal Squad Seven*. Anyway, we're going to shoot tomorrow. At the ranch. The writers figured out a way for the action to take place in our barn."

"It's an episode about space aliens!" said Abby, reading something off her phone. "Space aliens disguised as squirrels."

Jenny sighed. "Means I'm going to have to work with Nutty and Squiggy all night."

"But it's already nine o'clock," said Abby.

Jenny shrugged. "So I'll pull an all-nighter. If we lose *Dog Squad* . . ."

Abby finished the sentence for her. "We lose the ranch."

Jenny looked up into the rearview mirror. "Fred? We're going to need you to be Duke again."

"Boo-yah!" shouted Scruffy. "We're not breaking up the band!"

"Not yet, anyway," added Nala. "Oorah!"

Fred was thrilled. For a little while longer, he'd get to do more fun Duke stuff. He'd get to play make-believe with Nala and Scruffy. He'd get to help Jenny and Abby some more too!

The van pulled into the Second Chance Ranch.

"Here we are, guys," announced Jenny. "Home, sweet home."

The side door slid open. Jenny and Abby opened up the three crates.

"See you at the barn, first thing tomorrow," Scruffy said to Fred. "Maybe Jenny will let us sleep in a little, since, hello, the set is right over there."

"Get some rest, Fred," said Nala. "To stay in shape, rest is as important as working hard."

Nala and Scruffy trotted home to their bungalow. Fred went to his kennel. The one where he slept in the corner.

"Well, look who's back," said Cha-Cha.

"Hi, Cha-Cha," said Fred. "Hi, guys," he said to his other roommates.

"How was your time as a make-believe TV star?" Cha-Cha asked snidely.

"Wonderful," said Fred. "I got to pretend to drive a car and fly a helicopter and—"

"Save it," snipped the chow. "Nobody here really cares. We'd all rather hear about your big debut on Broadway, Fred. How you never even made it onstage because you were so afraid of the audience! It'd be a shame if something like that ever happened again."

Fred slumped to the floor and tucked his head between his legs. He could've told everybody the truth. How he'd rescued a scared young boy. How Cha-Cha had locked him out of the theater.

But why bother? Cha-Cha would just call him a liar.

Being Duke was a blast.

When it was time to go back to just being Fred?

That wouldn't be nearly as much fun.

EARLY THE NEXT morning, Fred, Nala, Scruffy, and Tater stood outside the barn, watching the scenery and prop people, who had worked through the night, load in the final set pieces.

The handyman, Mr. Babkow, and his son, Zachary, were helping.

Jenny was clutching a giant tumbler of coffee. She looked sleepy. She'd also been up all night—training the two squirrels who'd be in the scene with the dogs.

Abby led Fred, Nala, and Scruffy over to the awesome four-wheel all-terrain vehicles they'd be pretending to ride today. The costume people fitted them all with sleek, aerodynamic helmets (they had the official *Dog Squad* paw print shield on both sides).

"This is so cool," said Fred, admiring his ride.

"Wait till you do your first episode on a Jet Ski!" said Scruffy.

"Just be sure to wait an hour after eating before going into the water," added Nala. "Remember: safety is something that happens between your ears."

"So are headaches," cracked Scruffy.

"Are we ready to shoot?" asked the director.

"Ready!" Jenny shouted back with a yawn.

"Places, everyone. Quiet on the set. Roll camera. Aaaaaand action!"

EPISODE 3.7
"SQUIRRELS FROM OUTER SPACE"
SCENE 12

DUKE, NALA, AND Scruffy cruise up to the big red barn on their all-terrain vehicles.

Duke raises the tinted visor on his motorcycle helmet. Grim determination grips his face.

"That's where they led Tater," he whispers, his jaw firm.

"How can you be sure, Duke?" asks Scruffy.

"Easy." Duke points to a trail of broken nutshells leading to the barn doors. "Squirrels are messy eaters."

"Well, it's time we go in there and clean them up!" says Nala.

"Not so fast, my nimble friend," says Duke, holding up a paw. "If our intelligence is correct . . ."

"And it usually is," says Scruffy. "Those intelligence guys are very intelligent."

". . . then what we have feared for centuries is true. Squirrels aren't cute little nut-scavenging rodents. No, my friends. They are . . ."

There's a warbly sting of music like something out of a science fiction movie.

". . . aliens from another planet." Duke's voice echoes when he says it.

"Look, Duke!" says Nala, her laser-sharp eyes focused on a glimmering orb the size of a beach ball. "It's their spacecraft!"

Duke nods knowingly. "With acorn-powered propulsion."

"No wonder they're always gathering nuts!" says Scruffy. "They're not saving them for the winter! They're using them for their rocket ships."

"Helmets off," says Duke. "Ears up."

The three intrepid dogs remove their helmets and stealthily creep closer.

Meanwhile, inside the barn, the scrappy young puppy, Tater, is leashed to a post.

"How much did the young tail-wagger see?"

asks a squirrel in a shimmering silver space suit.

"Enough, Fearless Leader."

"I know you guys are from outer space!" yips Tater. "Oh yes you are."

"If word spreads," says the first squirrel, "it could jeopardize our eons-old plan to harvest nuts here on planet Earth."

"Then how would we fuel our fleet for the coming invasion?" demands the fearless leader.

Suddenly, Duke and Scruffy burst into the barn.

"How about with some of that hot gas you're blowing out your schnozzola?" snarls Scruffy.

"The game is up," says Duke, his head angled heroically. "We now know who you squirrels truly are. Extraterrestrial invaders from the Nutzoid Galaxy."

"That's why we dogs have been chasing you guys up trees for centuries!" adds Scruffy. "We had a hunch."

"I chased that squirrel," says Tater proudly. "The one with the chubby cheeks. He was snitching sunflower seeds out of a bird feeder even though he wasn't a bird."

"You did the right thing, Tater," Duke tells him.

"Oh, I quite agree," sneers the fearless leader, rubbing his tiny squirrel paws together with glee. "You did exactly the right thing, you puny-brained puppy. You brought my number one nemesis, Duke, to me and . . ."

There's a sting of DUN-DUN-DUN music.

". . . the Oblivion Flux Phaser!"

He gestures dramatically with his scrawny squirrel arm up to the hayloft, where a scary-looking ray-blasting cannon whirs to life. The rings of concentric circles along its barrel fluctuate through a rainbow of glowing colors as the weapon powers up.

"Whose game is up now, Dog Squad?" chirps the fearless leader.

"Oh no," Scruffy says nonchalantly to Duke. "Looks like we're in trouble."

"And when trouble calls . . . ," says Duke.

"It's Dog Squad to the rescue!" cries Nala, who has clambered undetected up to the rafters high above the barn floor. She leaps from her perch, deploys a tiny parachute, and executes a soft landing—straddling the thrumming ray gun as if it was a bucking bronco.

"She's pawsome!" barks Tater.

"I told you, kid," says Scruffy. "Nothin's too ruff for us."

"Take aim, Nala!" commands Duke.

Nala swivels the Oblivion Flux Phaser, tilts its barrel downward, and aims it directly at the two suddenly squeamish squirrels!

"We aim to please!" she announces calmly.

"Nuts!" cries the fearless leader, his eyes as wide as a flying saucer. "I don't feel so fearless anymore!"

"AAAAND CUT!" CRIED the director. "That's a wrap for today. Good work, everybody."

"You guys are so cool," said Tater.

"Thank you," said Nala, groaning a little.

"Are you okay?" Fred and Scruffy asked at the same time.

"Nothing serious," said Nala. "But that landing on the giant ray gun wasn't as soft as it might've appeared. I'm going to head over to the pool for a soak in the hot tub."

"Duke?" said Jenny.

She had to say it again because Fred wasn't used to people calling him that.

"Duke?"

Fred wagged his tail and gave her his full attention.

"We have a photographer here. We thought it'd be fun to get a shot of you with Squiggy and Nutty. Some with Tater, too."

"Ennn-joy," said Scruffy. "I'm gonna make sure Nala makes it to the hot tub okay."

"I'm fine," said Nala. "It's just a minor strain."

"Good. Let's just make sure it doesn't turn into a major pain. Like the original Duke."

"I'll catch up with you guys later," said Fred.

Scruffy and Nala headed through the trees to where the Second Chance Ranch had an amazing aboveground therapy pool for the dogs. They could either dive off the deck or walk down gently sloped ramps into the water. The Labradors did most of the diving. Everybody else used the ramps. There was also a hot tub for soaking sore muscles.

Fred trotted after Jenny and posed for a few quick snapshots with the two squirrels and Tater.

"Nap time," Abby announced to Tater when the photographer was finished.

"Aw, I don't want to take a nap!" Tater protested. But he was yawning when he did it.

"Get some rest, Tater," said Fred. "The Dog Squad needs you at your best."

"Okay, Duke," Tater said, hopping up into Abby's arms. "Whatever you say, Duke. You're the . . ."

He was asleep before he could finish that thought.

Fred chuckled. Duties complete, he scampered across the field and through the stand of trees bordering the swimming pool. He was a little sore too. Not Nala sore, but working on the show made his muscles ache. It was a good ache. The kind you get when you're having fun and not paying attention to how long you've been playing with your friends.

As he got closer to the pool, Fred heard burbling water and an angry voice off in the distance.

"He's doing what?" It was Duke. The real Duke.

Fred ducked down and peeked through the leaves of a tree.

Nala and Scruffy were relaxing in the hot tub. Duke was at the far end of the pool, sunning himself on the deck. There was a poodle serving him Frosty Paws ice cream from a paper tub.

"I said Fred's starring in two new episodes," Scruffy hollered back casually, as if it was no big deal. "In one, he gets to fly a helicopter."

"In the other," added Nala, "we turn the tables on alien invaders."

Duke rose up off his poolside lounger and stood on his wobbly legs.

"You shot two episodes without me?" Duke fumed. "Jenny and the others couldn't wait?"

"Nope," said Scruffy.

"The race goes to the swift," said Nala.

"You idiots can't do *Dog Squad* without me! I'm Duke. You two? You're nothing! You're nobodies."

Fred couldn't bear hearing Duke screaming at his friends the way Big Tony used to scream at Fred. He stepped onto the deck and joined his friends.

"Take it easy, Duke," he said. "It's only temporary.

When your leg's all better, you'll be Duke again. I'm just trying to help out. Because that's what families do. We help each other."

"Not in my family!" snarled Duke, his teeth flaring. "In my family, it's dog eat dog and every dog for himself! Where's Jenny? I need to bark some sense into Jenny!"

Duke was so riled up, he charged to the edge of the deck and dove off.

Unfortunately, he dove into the ramp, not the water.

Instead of a splash, there was a thud.

And a high-pitched yelp.

The ramp was made out of wood.

And Duke landed on it with all his legs splayed out.

When the vet left an hour later, he said Duke had broken two of them.

And rebroken the one he'd broken before.

With three legs wrapped in plaster casts, he wouldn't be able to work on *Dog Squad* for at least a month.

41

AROUND TWILIGHT THAT same day, Fred was playing fetch with Abby in the field near the barn.

"Hiya, Abby!" called Zachary Babkow. He was helping his dad and the TV crew break down the set inside the barn.

"Hiya, Zachary," Abby mumbled to her sneakers. She tossed the ball. Fred chased it.

"I thought Duke was injured," Fred heard Zachary say.

"Huh?"

Zachary pointed to Fred. "I heard Duke broke three legs. He heals quickly!"

"This isn't Duke," Abby replied softly as Fred brought back the slobbery rubber ball. "This is, uh, his stand-in. Fred."

"Oh, cool."

"Zachary?" called his father. "They need us inside."

"Catch you later, Abby."

Abby gave the boy, who clearly wanted to talk to her, another weak wave. "Later."

She sat down on the ground. That was Fred's cue to flop his head into her lap.

It reminded him of all the times he'd flopped his head into Susan's lap.

"I'm so worried," Abby told him. "Aunt Jenny is on a Zoom call with all the big shots at the network. She wants you to be Duke's permanent replacement."

Really? Fred's thought came out as a whimper. *Replace Duke? Permanently?*

"But what if the producers don't like the idea? The original Duke can't work for a month. What if they can't wait that long? What if they cancel the show instead? If we lose *Dog Squad*, we lose the ranch. It pays for everything else. The rescue work. The vet visits. Aunt Jenny wants to build a new kennel and take care of more strays."

Fred felt something buzz in Abby's pocket. Her phone. She pulled it out and checked the screen.

"It's Aunt Jenny," she said. "Hello?"

Fred could only hear Abby's side of the conversation.

"Really?"

Okay. Good. She sounded excited.

But there was a long, long pause.

"No way!"

Okay. Still good. Now she sounded super excited.

"Woo-hoo! I'll tell Fred."

Abby tapped her phone screen to end the call and hopped up to her feet.

"They love the idea! They absolutely love it!"

She heaved the ball. Fred chased it, brought it back, and dropped it into Abby's open palm.

"Aunt Jenny told them the truth. That it was *you* nailing every single take these last two episodes. *You* saving them so much time and money by being such a fast learner. *You* being so amazingly pawsome! So from now on, Fred, you're Duke! They're even going to use your name in the credits." She ran her free hand across the sky as if she was scanning a movie marquee. "It's going to be *Dog Squad Starring Fred as Duke!*"

She flung the ball toward the barn. Fred trotted off to retrieve it. Not very swiftly because his mind was the part of his body currently racing.

I'm going to be the forever Duke? Even when Duke gets better? They're going to tell people my name? I won't just be pretending to be Duke—I'll actually be Duke?

Fred picked up the ball but didn't immediately run it back to Abby. Because Zachary had just come out of the barn, wiping his hands on his dusty jeans.

Fred had a thought. A way to help Abby talk to Zachary, because—you didn't have to be a human psychic to know it—that was what both of them wanted.

So he took the ball to Zachary instead of Abby.

Zachary could've tossed it back to Abby. He could've thrown it for Fred. Instead, he did what Fred had hoped he would do.

He started walking toward Abby.

"Is this yours?" he said, holding out the ball.

"Yeah," said Abby. "Well, technically, I guess it's Fred's. I don't, you know, chase rubber balls. Not as a rule."

"Yeah," Zachary said with a laugh, "me neither."

Fred ambled behind Zachary as the nice boy moved closer to Abby.

"So, what does a stand-in do?" asked Zachary.

"Huh?"

"You said Fred here was Duke's stand-in."

"Not anymore. Now he's Duke!"

It was Zachary's turn to say, "Huh?"

Abby plopped down on the grass. "It's kind of a long story."

"I have time." Zachary sat down beside her. "We're all finished in the barn."

Fred lay down and put his head back in Abby's lap so she could pet it while she talked to a good boy who wasn't a dog.

"Okay," said Abby, taking a deep breath. "Duke's injured, so Fred's going to be Duke. It's like that old movie where the understudy goes on for the big star after she breaks her leg or whatever. They're going to promote it big-time because people love an underdog story! And in this story, the underdog is a real dog. Of course, the original Duke will always have a home here at the ranch. And the finest vet care . . ."

As Abby rambled on, Fred drifted off for a snooze with his head cradled in her lap.

She didn't really need Fred's help to talk to Zachary anymore.

Once she got going, she did just fine on her own.

"WE'RE GOING TO the Scoop Sloop for ice cream cones" were the words Fred woke to.

He'd been napping on Abby's lap for over an hour. Now she and Zachary wanted to head down to Atlantic Avenue. They couldn't do that with Fred's head on Abby's lap.

Fred stood up, shook himself awake.

"You better get some rest," Abby told him. "Tomorrow's another big day."

"Here," said Zachary, handing Fred the squishy rubber ball. "I believe this is yours."

Fred took the ball, gave Zachary and Abby a tail wag, and headed toward the kennels.

But he wasn't going to his. Not right away. He wanted to make a stop.

No, he *needed* to make that stop.

He had to make sure he was the one who told Tater

the truth. He did not want to disappoint or disillusion Tater, the way the real Duke had disillusioned Fred.

He also remembered the lies Susan had told when she turned Fred over to the animal shelter. How her boyfriend was allergic to Fred. How Fred was a "biter." That Fred was "just too aggressive." Huh. Maybe that was why Big Tony had wanted him.

Lies never led to anything good. It was like Nala said in the *Dog Squad* episode where they exposed a bunch of quill-and-ink art forgeries done by a very talented porcupine: "The truth doesn't cost anything. But a lie could cost you everything."

Fred went to the building where the puppy was bunking.

"Tater? You got a minute?"

"For you, Duke? You betcha."

Fred sighed. "That's just it, Tater. I wanted you to hear this from me before you heard it from someone else."

Probably Cha-Cha, he thought.

"Hear what?"

"I haven't been honest with you, Tater. I'm not Duke. I'm Fred."

"Huh?"

"That other dog, the one who leapt off the dock and hurt himself?"

Tater nodded. "I saw him when the vet came. He looks just like you, Duke. You guys could be twins!"

"I know. But that dog with all the broken legs is the real Duke. I'm just Fred. His double. Jenny asked me to fill in for him after he was hurt the first time. But now Duke is injured again. They want me to take over. They want me to become the new Duke. But the truth is, I'm nothing special, Tater. I'm not a superstar or a superhero. I'm just a dog, like you. An ordinary dog with an ordinary name. I'm just Fred."

Tater stared at Fred. Panting. His eyes wide.

I've broken his tiny little heart, Fred thought. *Tater's going to hate me. I wouldn't blame him. You can't build a friendship (or a family) on lies.*

Finally, Tater said something.

"You *are* something special, Fred! Remember? On the beach? You saved me from that—"

"Shhh," said Fred. "That's still our secret."

"Right. Gotcha. And you're still my hero, Duke. I mean Fred."

"I wouldn't be surprised if you were in even more shows too."

"Really?" said Tater. "Wow. That's exciting."

"I'm excited too," said Fred. "But I'm also afraid."

"I bet you are! I sure would be! I'd be terrified! Wait a second. I *am* terrified. I'm going to be in more shows? That's scary!"

"Well," said Fred, "as a wise old soul once told me,

'true courage means you're scared but you go ahead and do what needs to be done anyway.'"

"Oh. Okay. I can do it. But only if you do it with me. You're going to be Duke. Right, Fred?"

Fred smiled. He thought about Jenny and Abby, Nala and Scruffy. Everyone who'd believed in him and was now counting on him.

"I'm sure gonna try."

THE NEXT MORNING, Fred, Nala, and Scruffy were eating breakfast together in a shady spot on the deck behind Jenny's house.

Jenny was sharing coffee and bagels with the *Dog Squad* creator, Leo Espinosa, at the nearby picnic table.

"Our next episode is going to take place in New York City!" said Leo.

"Okay," said Jenny. "The dogs can stay at the Brooklyn town house we use for our Broadway dogs."

"We'll have a really early call. It might be better if we rent a hotel closer to the set."

"Where are we shooting?"

"A place called Shinbone Alley. Very seedy, very scary. That's where the kidnappers will have their lair."

"Kidnappers?"

"Right. But first, the Dog Squad has to travel from their secret hideout to the big city."

"How do they travel this time?" asked Jenny. "Chopper? Private jet? Submarine?"

Fred hoped he'd get to drive that tire-screeching car again.

Leo shook his head. "No. This is better. They're in a hurry. They get word, at the very last minute, from Tater, that a purebred chow chow, the top contender for Best in Show at the International Dog Show, is going to be kidnapped."

"We have a chow chow named Cha-Cha," said Jenny.

"Ha! Funny! We'll use that name in the script. Anyway, Duke and the squad don't have time for their usual elaborate plans. This is an emergency. They have to hop on the next train to New York City!"

"And how will they do that?" said Jenny.

"Easy. They sneak onto a commuter train. The train pulls in. Its doors slide open. Duke, Scruffy, and Nala hop through the doors just as they're sliding shut."

"This is good," Scruffy said to Duke and Nala.

"Some of Mr. Espinosa's finest work," agreed Nala.

Leo showed Jenny a storyboard sketching out the action shots.

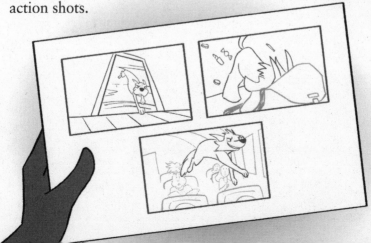

"Once they're in New York, they find where Cha-Cha is being held: a seedy warehouse just off an even seedier alley. They work out their plan and rescue her. Cha-Cha makes it to the dog show, just in the nick of time, and wins Best in Show. Scruffy makes a wisecrack: 'Next year, we should enter the working dogs competition. Because we work harder than any dogs I know!'"

"Oooh," said Scruffy. "Good line."

"I like the jumping into the train," said Nala.

"I'm just glad we save the day," said Fred.

"Get used to it, pal," said Scruffy. "Day saving? It's what we do best!"

"OKAY," SAID JENNY, who'd started jotting down notes in a small spiral notebook. "This will be great."

"Let's take the dogs to the train station tomorrow," said Leo. "You and the director can work out the blocking and stunts. We'll shoot the train-hopping scene on Saturday. I have a feeling America is going to love our new Duke even more than I do."

"I guess we'll find out tonight," said Jenny. "It's Thursday. Fred's first episode streams at eight."

"And by nine? He's going to be a star!"

Abby led Fred back to the kennel he shared with a dozen other dogs, including, of course, Cha-Cha.

Abby unclipped Fred's leash and went over to Cha-Cha.

"Have you heard the news?" she said cheerfully. "You're going to guest-star in the next episode of *Dog Squad.*"

"About time," said Cha-Cha. All Abby heard was a happy yap.

"I'm picking up some very strong happiness signals," said Abby, putting her fingertips to her temples. "You'll be great, Cha-Cha. Fred can give you a few pointers. After all, he's Duke. Now and forever!"

As soon as Abby was gone, Cha-Cha turned to Fred.

"*You*'re Duke?" she snickered. "You're not just a part-timer filling in for the real Duke? Impossible."

Fred was so tired of Cha-Cha needling him. He wondered why some dogs only felt good when they made others feel bad. He decided to gloat a little. Not a lot. Just a little.

"It's true," he said. "Now that Duke has reinjured himself, they want me to take over for him. Permanently."

For the first time since they'd met, Cha-Cha was speechless. She stood there with her mouth open and her purple tongue dangling out.

"Now, if you will excuse me," said Fred, "I need to go take a nap. My first episode streams tonight and we're having a party at Jenny's place to celebrate."

THAT EVENING, ABBY took Fred up to Jenny's house to watch his *Dog Squad* premiere.

"Zachary is going to be at the party," Abby said. "His dad, too." Abby didn't sound nervous or shy. In fact, she sounded happy.

Mission accomplished.

The house was packed. Fred recognized a lot of the people from the show, all of them holding plastic cups filled with something bubbly and nibbling small human treats off party platters. Fred joined Scruffy, Nala, Tater, and Clarence, the cat, in front of the TV set.

Where Clarence didn't stay for long.

There was an empty cardboard carton in the kitchen that'd caught his attention.

"Later," he said, strutting off to curl up and nap inside the box.

"This is so exciting," said Tater. "We're going to be on TV, Fred!"

Fred tried to smile. But he was nervous. What if he was a lousy Duke?

"Shhh, everybody," said Jenny as music swelled and the dramatic *Dog Squad* opening filled the screen.

"Welcome to *Dog Squad*!" boomed the announcer. "With Scruffy, Nala, and, tonight, starring Fred as Duke! When trouble calls, it's Dog Squad to the rescue!"

The humans all applauded. Fred and his friends barked. The hourlong episode was action-packed from minute one.

"You're awesome, Fred!" cried Scruffy.

"No," said Nala, "he's pawsome!"

Fred felt a rush of excitement and pride like he'd never felt before.

"You guys are all great too!" he told his friends.

"True," said Scruffy. "We are. But you're the star, Fred!"

Apparently, America agreed. Before the show was over, all the humans were checking their buzzing and binging phones.

They liked what they saw.

"Best episode ever!" said an executive from the streaming company. She rattled off a bunch of numbers that the other humans cheered.

"Listen to this!" shouted Leo. "It's a post from the *Times* TV critic. 'The two new dogs, the intrepid Fred as Duke and the beyond-cute puppy Tater, just stole this country's heart. Tonight, two new dog stars lit up the night.'"

There was more celebrating and congratulating.

Finally, when it was nearly midnight, Jenny jokingly

announced that she was "kicking everybody out" of her house.

"We have a big day tomorrow, folks. We'll be taking the dogs over to the Wilford station to rehearse the train-jumping scene. Go home. Get some rest!"

Nala and Scruffy said good night to Fred and Tater, then headed off to the bungalow they shared with Reginald. Zachary and Mr. Babkow were the last to leave. Fred smiled as he watched Abby and Zachary cleaning up paper plates, napkins, and cups. Everyone needed a friend, and he was glad Abby had found one.

After the Babkows went home, Abby led Fred and Tater across the open field to Fred's kennel.

"How about you bunk with Fred tonight, Tater?" Abby said. "Your thoughts are coming in loud and clear. You're afraid. Don't be. You're going to be great in the train scene tomorrow."

"I've got your back, Tater," said Fred. "Nala and Scruffy, too."

"Thanks, Duke! I mean Fred."

"Huh," said Abby, doing a quick bed check in the kennel. "Cha-Cha's not here. Guess she stepped outside to use the bathroom. G'night, everybody. Sweet dreams."

When Abby left the kennel, Tater turned to Fred.

"I'm glad I get to sleep with you tonight, Fred, because Abby's right. She really read my mind. I was thinking about everybody saying I was a TV star and all I could think was *I'm afraid!* Because I've never been a TV star before. And Abby heard it, word for word."

Fred arched a skeptical eyebrow. He still had his doubts about Abby's mind-reading capabilities. But she did seem to have a special connection with Tater. Maybe because he was still a puppy. His thoughts were probably very, very loud and very, very energetic.

CHA-CHA CREPT THROUGH the shadows, making her way toward Duke's private doghouse.

She hadn't been invited to Fred's big premiere party at Jenny's house. She had, however, snuck over, peeked through the patio doors, and listened. It was some celebration.

I'm sure there will be an even bigger party when my episode airs, she told herself. *In fact, I wouldn't be surprised if they rethought the whole show once America swoons over Cha-Cha the chow chow. Yes. That'll be the show's new name:* Cha-Cha the Chow Chow.

But if Jenny and the others stuck with the silly *Dog Squad* premise, Cha-Cha would be reduced to making one guest appearance. Unless, of course, the star of the show made certain demands. She knew Fred would never ask for anything special. He was too humble. Too . . . "nice."

But Duke? The original? The true star?

He could throw a tantrum or two until Jenny figured out what he wanted: Cha-Cha to costar in every episode! But to earn that favor, Cha-Cha would have to do a favor for Duke first.

She padded up the ramp to Duke's doggy door and stuck in her head.

"Duke? Are you home? Sorry about the late hour . . ."

"Go away," growled Duke. "I have a cone the size of a lampshade on my head and I can't lick myself!"

"I won't be long," said Cha-Cha, slathering her voice with butter. "By the way, I'm a huge fan."

"So?"

"So, I want to help you."

"Help me? Ha. How can a purple-tongued fur mop like you help me? I'm Duke!"

"Yes. You were."

"Huh?"

"Oh, I'm sorry. Perhaps you haven't heard."

"I haven't heard what?"

"That Jenny Yen has replaced you. Permanently."

"What?"

"That fraud Fred has stolen your show," Cha-Cha continued. "His first episode aired tonight. And oh, how the humans gushed about him. Did you know that they're now introducing the show as *Dog Squad Starring Fred as Duke*?"

"What? They can't do that. *I'm* Duke!"

Duke rose and stumbled forward on his wobbly, plaster-caked limbs. Then he tumbled, sideways, to the floor.

"Duke?" said Cha-Cha, sounding as compassionate and caring as she could possibly pretend to be. "Sometimes even heroes need a little help. Like when their bones are broken. Or their head is stuck inside a plastic cone. That's a good time to ask for help."

"From who?"

"Me. I'm willing to do you a favor if, in return, you, one day, do a small favor for me."

"What's the favor you're gonna give me? That's the only one I'm interested in."

"Of course. Of course. I know Fred's weaknesses. I've studied his fears. I know how to play mind games and make him mess up so much they'll be begging for you to come back!"

"Seriously?"

"Imagine what might happen if Fred freaked out while the cameras were rolling? If he slowed things down. If he threatened the future of *Dog Squad*. Why, I imagine Jenny might regret her decision to replace you."

"You can make that happen?"

"Oh, yes. I'm very skilled at psychological warfare. And I've just been cast in the next episode of *Dog Squad*. I'll have plenty of opportunities to mess with Fred's head."

"And what's the favor you want from me?"

"Nothing, really. Nothing at all. Just a chance to co-star with you on a regular basis. Oh, did I mention that Nala and Scruffy love, love, *love* working with Fred?"

Duke growled.

"I agree," said Cha-Cha. "I think, when you come back to save the show, you should dump them both and find a new sidekick—me!"

47

BIG TONY BOMBOLONI and his dogs came home so late on Thursday night that it was actually Friday morning.

"You two stink," he told Dozer and Petunia. "You'll never make it as guard dogs."

Big Tony had taken the dogs to an abandoned warehouse where he could work on their "intruder attack" skills. He'd put on a big padded suit that he'd made out of pillows, a tattered movers' blanket, and a pair of puffy winter parkas. In that night's drill, the dogs were sup-

posed to spring at him and latch on to his limbs with their snarling teeth.

Instead, they aimed for his butt.

"We don't want to be no guard dogs!" growled Dozer.

"We want food!" added Petunia. "Somethin' better than the garbage this guy keeps feeding us. The stuff in the dumpster was better. More gravy."

Dozer rolled his eyes. "That wasn't gravy, Petunia, that was . . . Oh, never mind!"

"You two were supposed to make me rich," griped Big Tony. He tossed a pair of dented metal bowls on the floor and filled them with cut-rate kibble from a bargain bag. "You know what a *good* guard dog goes for these days? I'll tell you. There's a German shepherd on the internet on sale for fifty-five thousand dollars. For one dog! Fifty-five K!"

"What a sleazeball," muttered Dozer.

"What do I gotta do to motivate you two?" Big Tony wondered aloud. "Have I been working you too hard? You want a reward? You want to stream tonight's brand-new episode of *Dog Squad*?"

"Of course, you idiot," said Petunia. "We're dogs!"

All Big Tony heard was a sharp bark and an angry snarl.

"All right, already!"

He clicked on the TV and thumbed the remote to find the *Dog Squad* playback.

"Watch your show. I'm hungry. I think I have a slice of mushroom pizza in the fridge from last week."

He pressed the Play button and headed for the creaky staircase.

"Welcome to *Dog Squad*!" boomed the TV. "With Scruffy, Nala, and, tonight, starring Fred as Duke!"

Big Tony froze on the second step.

"Fred?"

He spun around and raced back to the TV. He swiveled the screen so he could glare at it.

"That's him. That's my dog. Fred! They stole my dog and put him on TV? Oh, somebody's gonna pay for this. They're gonna pay lots and lots of money. And guess what? They're gonna pay it all to me!"

48

FIRST THING FRIDAY morning, Abby gave Fred a bubble bath and blowout.

He had to look his fluffiest because second thing Friday morning, he would appear, live, on the *Today* show with Jenny to talk about the big changes on *Dog Squad*.

"I'm so glad we found you," said Abby as she combed out Fred's fur.

Fred beamed. He was glad too.

"You know, Fred, in the six years I've lived with Aunt Jenny, I've met a lot of dogs. Guess what? You just might be my favorite."

Wow, thought Fred. Nobody had ever told him anything like that before. Not even Susan. He was kind of getting choked up.

"I saw a poster once in a gift shop," Abby continued. "It said 'Home is not a place, it's a feeling.' I like that. Because home is how I feel when I'm with Aunt Jenny and all you guys. I hope this feels like home to you, too, Fred."

It sure did. For the first time, he was almost glad that Susan had given him up. Sure, it had hurt at the time, but maybe it was just part of the journey that would eventually lead him to Jenny, Abby, and this warm, cozy feeling of home.

FOR THE TV interviews, Jenny and Fred sat in front of a wall filled with *Dog Squad* graphics and talked to a camera, since they were still in Connecticut and the TV people were wherever TV people lived.

After the *Today* show, they did *Good Morning America, Fox & Friends,* and *Breakfast Time TV.* When they were done doing their TV chats, Fred and Jenny joined Abby, Scruffy, Nala, and Tater for the ride to the Wilford train station and rehearsal.

"Everybody secure?" Jenny asked.

"Secure!" replied Abby.

But before Jenny could start up the van, her phone started chirping. She tapped a button on the dashboard that put the call on the car's speakers.

"This is Jenny Yen," she said.

"Aha! Gotcha!" said the caller.

Fred immediately recognized the voice. And he wasn't happy to hear it.

"Are you okay, Fred?" whispered Tater. "Because you don't look so okay. You look kind of queasy. . . ."

"It took me a while to track you people down," chortled the caller.

"Who is this?" asked Jenny.

"Name's Tony Bomboloni."

Fred gulped. He'd been right. It was Big Tony!

"That dog you people are using in your TV show? The new star of *Dog Squad*. Fred? The one on all the talk shows this morning? He's mine."

"Sir, I think you called the wrong number."

"Was he wearing a collar when you nabbed him? A collar with his name spelled out on it?"

"Mr. Bomboloni, I don't think—"

"How'd you know his name was Fred if you didn't read it off his collar?"

Jenny looked at Abby. Fred saw a flicker of fear in Abby's eyes. She nodded and mimed spelling *F-R-E-D* on her neck.

"I'm the one what wrote his name on that collar," Big Tony continued. "Used a Sharpie. *F-R-E-D*. Fred."

Fred knew that was a lie. Susan had made the collar, not Big Tony. But it didn't really matter. The collar was proof that Fred had "belonged" to other people before he found his home with Jenny and Abby.

"I got pictures, too. Lots and lots of pictures. Me and Fred. Fred and me . . ."

"Mr. Bomboloni?" said Jenny, her muscles rippling as she squeezed the steering wheel hard. "We adopted Fred from the New York City Animal Control Center. They informed us that Fred had been abandoned in an alleyway. That he showed signs of neglect, maybe even abuse . . ."

"Yeah, well, that was before he was streaming all over Disney Plus. Now? Why, I'd treat him like the big-shot star he is."

"Mr. Bomboloni? This conversation is over. If you wish to pursue this matter further, I suggest you hire a lawyer."

"Bad suggestion. I can't afford no lawyer. So I suggest we cut a deal. You pay me, say, fifty-five thou for my dog plus a little extra for the collar you stole plus some more for all my pain and suffering."

"Good day, Mr. Bomboloni."

"You ain't heard the last of me, lady!"

"I said, good day!" Jenny jabbed the dashboard button. The call was over. Fred worried that his new life might be over too.

COULD BIG TONY *really drag me back to that dark cellar where I lived all alone and didn't have any friends, let alone a family?* Fred worried.

"Do you know that man?" asked Nala.

"He's scary-sounding," said Tater. "I hope I never meet him. He'd scare me."

"Ah, don't worry about it," said Scruffy. "Jenny will take care of it. She takes care of everything. Once I had this rash—"

"Never forget," said Nala, "you're one of us now, Fred. You too, Tater. You both belong to team *Dog Squad*. Nothin's too ruff for us!"

"Nala?" said Scruffy. "How many times have I got to tell you? That's my catchphrase, not yours."

"I believe Mr. Leo Espinosa said it first," said Nala. "In a script."

"He may have written the words," said Scruffy. "But I gave it the zazz!"

"Come on, guys," said Jenny, cranking the ignition. "We need to be at the train station. We've got some rehearsing to do."

"And training!" cracked Scruffy. "At the train station! We're gonna *train* at the *train* station!"

Nala rolled her eyes while Fred and Tater chuckled.

Yeah, thought Fred. *It's good to be part of something bigger than myself. It's good to be part of a family.*

IT WAS A Friday afternoon, so the train platform was nearly empty.

A few midday travelers waited patiently at the Wilford station for the 2:33 to New York. The director was holding up her hands, framing the shots she'd like to see. Leo was scribbling furiously in a notebook.

"Great!" he said when she saw Jenny and Abby leading the dogs up a set of steps. "Here come our stars."

"Hiya, guys," said Abby.

"Beautiful day," added Jenny.

"Hope it's like this tomorrow when we shoot," said Leo. "Okay, here's the setup. We start the scene with Tater looking up at Duke, Nala, and Scruffy with his big brown eyes. 'You have to find Cha-Cha!' Tater tells them. 'Her rival's evil owner kidnapped her.'"

"Then," said the director, "the three *Dog Squad* dogs peel off. Each one finds a random commuter to pretend to say goodbye to. We'll need the dogs standing exactly where a set of doors will open and—"

A train rumbling into the station blew its air horn.

"Hang on," said Leo. "Here comes the two-thirty-three."

"Back up, everybody," suggested Abby. She scooped up Tater and cradled him in her arms. Fred stepped back from the edge of the platform too.

The commuter train hissed its brakes and screech-squealed to a stop. Doors in the middles of all the cars, except the last one, slid open with a whir and a BONG! chime.

A few people streamed out. Others shuffled in.

"This station stop is Wilford," Fred heard a recorded voice announce. "Wilford."

At the far end of the platform, a conductor waved his arms over his head.

"All aboard!" he bellowed. "Use all doors except those in the rear car of the train. The rear car is closed. All aboard!"

"Hey, look, you guys!" said Tater, panting eagerly. "See that lady on the train with a dog in her purse? I know her. Not the lady. The dog. That's Jasmine. From the Coastal Animal Shelter. That's where I was! Hey, Jasmine? Yoo-hoo! It's me! Tater!"

With a burst of puppy rocket fuel, Tater sprang out of Abby's arms and flew into the train.

Abby shrieked.

"Tater!" shouted Fred.

The doors slid shut.

The train started to pull out of the station.

Jenny sprang into action. "Conductor?" She raced down the platform, looking for someone to stop the train.

She couldn't find anybody.

Fred's heart beat faster. Tater was on his way to New York City! It could be a dangerous place. Dogs like Dozer and Petunia lurked in all the shadows, ready to pounce. What if somebody like Big Tony grabbed the puppy?

"We've got to save Tater!" Fred hollered.

"How?" said Scruffy.

"I'm not sure!"

Fred took off running. He chased the train as it picked up speed.

"Whoa!" said Scruffy. "Come back! We're actors! We can't really do heroic stuff!"

"Speak for yourself!" cried Nala. She tore down the platform after Fred.

"Oh, great," said Scruffy, sprinting after Nala and Fred. "I always wanted to catch a train to New York."

"Fred?" shouted Jenny. "Stop! Heel!"

"Save Tater!" cried Abby. "He's scared. I can feel it!"

"Abby?" pleaded Jenny. "This is no time for a psychic reading!"

The train was nearing the end of the elevated platform.

Fred could obey Jenny's command. He could skid to a stop.

Or he could save his friend.

Suddenly, the rear exit on the very last car swung open. Someone must've left it unlatched. Maybe it was broken. Maybe that was why the conductor had said the rear car was closed. Or maybe the train was just trying to tell Fred what he needed to do!

Sorry, Jenny, he thought. *But a dog's gotta do what a dog's gotta do!*

FRED LEAPT ONTO the moving train in a single bound.

Nala and Scruffy jumped in right behind him.

"Where's Tater?" asked Nala, sweeping the empty car with her eyes.

"The next car, I think," said Fred. "I can smell him."

Scruffy sniffed the air. "Puppies smell good. Like fresh-baked dog biscuits."

"If Tater's in the next car," said Nala, "what're we doing back here?"

"Nala's right," said Fred. "Let's go, you guys!"

"Dog Squad to the rescue!" shouted Scruffy.

Fred led the way up the empty train car's aisle.

The door at the far end swung open. A big man in a blue uniform and boxy hat blocked the exit. The conductor.

"What're you dogs doing back here?" he demanded.

"We were just asking ourselves the same thing," cracked Scruffy. To the conductor, his wisecrack sounded like a snippy yap.

"Quick!" said Nala. "The door into the next car hasn't slid shut yet!"

She flew up the aisle, scooting between the conductor's legs as if he was a tunnel on an obstacle course.

The conductor spun around. His body blocked the path to the door.

What would Nala do? Fred thought quickly. And then he did it.

He hopped up into a nearby seat, sprang forward, and vaulted over the tops of all the other seat backs like an Olympic hurdler.

Meanwhile, Scruffy did what he did best. He snapped and snarled and yapped at the conductor. The conductor started dancing a jig so Scruffy couldn't latch on to the cuffs of his uniform pants and yank them down.

With the conductor distracted, Fred and Nala had time to search the next car. It was packed.

"There!"

Fred saw Tater, maybe a dozen seats up. He looked scared. The foo-foo dog in the lady's purse was snarling at him.

Fred and Nala barked to get Tater's attention.

"Tater!"

"It's us!"

"Help!" Tater yipped back.

"Shhhh!" said one of the passengers. "This is the quiet car. No barking allowed."

"Sorry," Fred said quietly.

He and Nala made their way to Tater.

"That's not Jasmine," said the puppy. "I thought it was, but it's not. I did a really dumb thing, didn't I?"

"It wasn't your wisest move," said Nala. "But sometimes mistakes are the best teachers. We can learn from them."

"I want to learn to be like Fred!"

The tiny dog in the purse growled some more.

Finally, the train slowed as it pulled into the next station. The conductor marched into the car, carrying Scruffy by the scruff of his neck.

"Um, you guys?" said Scruffy. "I have a funny feeling that, wherever we are, this is going to be our final stop."

THE NEXT STOP was Bradford, Connecticut.

And that was where Fred, Nala, Scruffy, and Tater were shown the door.

"Get off my train!" hollered the conductor. "And stay off!" He sounded so grouchy Fred had to wonder if the headband on his boxy hat was a little too snug.

"That was some workout!" said Nala as the four dogs trotted down a set of steps to a sea of cars lined up in a parking lot. "Very invigorating. Good idea, Fred."

"Yeah," said Scruffy. "Except for that first bit. The jumping onto the train part. I've got stubby legs. I don't like leaping."

"Thanks for rescuing me, you guys," said Tater.

"In the future, Tater," suggested Nala, "let's try to stick to the script. Improvising can be dangerous."

"So. How do we get back to Jenny?" asked Fred.

"We could bark at people," said Scruffy. "Eventually,

one of them will read our dog tags. The tags have Jenny's phone number."

"Good idea," said Fred.

Fred led the way across the commuter parking lot to Main Street. The others followed him, with Nala bringing up the rear so she could corral Tater if he started wandering off again.

As they roamed in a tight pack up the sidewalk, people started recognizing them.

"Look, Mom!" shouted a boy. "It's Duke and the dogs from *Dog Squad*."

"And that's Tater Tot!" cried a girl. "He's the cutest! I want a stuffed Tater for my birthday!"

"Yikes!" screeched Tater. "I don't want to be stuffed."

"Take it easy, kid," said Scruffy. "She's talking about a cuddly toy that looks like you."

"Nobody wants to really stuff you," Fred reassured Tater.

"Phew. That's a relief."

A crowd started to form. Selfies were snapped. Paws were shaken. Fred said hello with his friendly smile to all his admirers and gave a few a sloppy kisses on the cheek.

Before long, the commotion drew the attention of a police cruiser. The two officers stepped out of their car.

"Hey, look," said one. "It's Duke."

"And Nala," said the other. "I *love* Nala."

They took their own selfies and then called the phone number printed on all the tags jingling off the dogs' collars.

"Fred?" gushed Tater as the four dogs received head pats and ear rubs. "You're my hero, you know that, right?"

Jenny, on the other hand, wasn't so happy when she and Abby arrived to collect the dogs.

"You could've hurt yourself," she scolded Fred as she ushered him into his crate. "You could've hurt Scruffy and Nala, too. We would've gone after Tater. You're not a superhero, Fred. You're just a dog who looks a lot like the other dog who used to play Duke!"

Fred had never heard Jenny sound so upset.

Then again, he'd never done anything so dangerous or, now that he thought about it, so stupid.

Who did he think he was?

ON SATURDAY, WHEN they shot the train scene for real, Fred was on his best behavior.

He didn't do anything until Jenny showed him exactly what she wanted him to do. He stuck to the script. He hit his marks. He did the actions Jenny had trained him to do; no more, no less.

By the early afternoon, Jenny was telling Fred he was a "good boy. Such a good, good boy."

In between takes, Jenny worked with Cha-Cha, who'd come to the train station location to learn her moves for the upcoming scenes in the warehouse down in New York City.

By five, the director had everything she needed. "Okay, that's a wrap on this location," she announced. "Tater is done for this episode. He can head home. Good work today, guys. And thanks for not chasing any trains, Fred." She gave Fred's fur a good rub. "We need to transport Fred,

Scruffy, and Nala down to New York tomorrow. We'll need the chow chow, too. When we're in the city, I want to move quickly, people. The weather forecast doesn't look great for next week. There's a storm blowing up the coast that could turn into a hurricane. I'd love to have all our exterior shots finished by Tuesday. What's the chow's name again?"

"Cha-Cha," said Abby.

"Oh. Right. Cha-Cha the chow chow. Duh. How come I keep forgetting that?"

CHA-CHA HEARD THE director say that.

She had been napping near the semicircle of canvas-backed chairs where the production big shots sat, because she was exhausted. Jenny had been working her hard between train scene takes.

But now the director had her full attention.

You'd better remember my name, lady, she fumed. *Because when I'm done with Fred and these other amateurs, I'm going to be this show's newest and biggest star!*

★DIRECT

53

AS SOON AS they got back to Jenny's place, Cha-Cha
slipped away to visit Duke.

The *real* Duke!

"What's the report?" Duke demanded, attempting,
once again, to shake off the irritating plastic collar tied
around his neck.

"Oh, it's juicy!" said Cha-Cha, wriggling her ears
knowingly.

"Quit wriggling your ears. You're such a fur face I can
hardly see 'em anyhow. Tell me what's going on!"

"You mean who might get canned from the show if he
keeps messing up?"

"Cha-Cha?"

"Yes, Duke?"

"I'm not like the fools who watch my show. I don't
like suspense. Cut to the chase."

"Very well. Cut to the chase I shall. That fraud Fred is skating on thin ice."

"Really? I did that in season two. I saved a poodle in the middle of a frozen pond. I had to wear specially built skates."

"I'm sorry," said Cha-Cha. "I should've been more specific. I meant to say that Fred has been making some risky moves that are seriously jeopardizing his future on *Dog Squad*. One more and I feel quite certain they'll be begging you to come back."

"I can't, you idiot. These casts won't come off for three more weeks!"

"Trust me, Duke. They'll delay new episodes until you're better if we—or rather, I—can encourage Fred to make a few more embarrassing blunders."

"They really want me back?"

"Not yet. But they will. Oh, you should've heard what they were saying around the playback monitors on the set today. I certainly did. I pretended to be napping, but I picked up everything!"

"What? What'd they say?"

"Apparently, Fred pulled a dangerous stunt at the train station yesterday."

"What'd he do?"

"He hopped on a moving train!"

"So? It was probably an action sequence."

"No, Duke. This leap wasn't in the script. Fred just

jumped on a train for no reason. 'The real Duke would never do anything that dangerous,' the director said."

Duke smiled. "They really miss me, huh?"

"Oh, you bet they do. And they're going to miss you even more when Fred has his Monday-morning meltdown."

"How's that gonna happen?"

"When we shoot our scenes together, I'm going to mess with his head. When I'm done with Fred, I guarantee you he won't be able to sit, stay, roll over, or even remember his name!"

NALA AND SCRUFFY were thrilled to be spending a few nights in New York City.

Fred? Not so much. New York was home to Big Tony, and he couldn't stop thinking about that phone call.

"Ah, it's good to be back in the big city!" Cha-Cha said when the four dogs assembled in the lobby of their hotel first thing Monday morning.

Abby was holding all their leashes while they waited for Jenny to grab a "quick cup of coffee" before walking over to the set.

"You remember New York and Broadway, don't you, Fred? How you wandered off and missed your only entrance? Sure hope you don't do something like that again."

"Yo, Cha-Cha?" said Scruffy. "Zip your lips. If you can find 'em, fur face."

Nala chuckled. "Good one, Scruffy."

They pawed each other a high five.

Jenny came over, sipping her coffee and consulting her phone.

"Okay, that tropical storm is now officially Hurricane Adelaide. They say it'll hit us in a few days. Or it could turn east and head out to sea."

"If we move fast," said Abby, "we might be able to finish all our setups in one day."

"It's possible, I guess," said Jenny. She smiled at the four dogs. "No mistakes today, guys. If we nail everything on the first take, we can head home later tonight. If not, we'll need to spend another night in the city."

"I wouldn't mind a few more nights in the hotel," said Cha-Cha. "The free shampoo and conditioner are splendid. How about you, Fred? Think we'll need to spend an extra day or two waiting for the search party to bring you back from wherever you wander off to this time?"

"All right, Ms. Cha-Cha-Cha," growled Scruffy. "That's enough."

"More than enough," roared Nala.

"He's Duke!" snapped Scruffy. "Remember that and show some respect, you purple-tongued, orange-furred cheese puff!"

"You guys?" said Abby, tugging on the jostling dogs' leashes. "I know you're all super excited to go to work, but you need to settle down."

"Come on," said Jenny as she closed the weather app on her phone. "They need us on the set."

Jenny and Abby walked the dogs over to their first location, which was only a few blocks from the hotel. It was a place the script called Shinbone Alley, in a shabby section of the city.

It was a part of town Fred knew very well.

Because it was the same alley he'd been tossed into by Big Tony. In fact, Fred could see his old home. The dirt-smeared windows looking down into its basement were right where the crew was setting up to shoot the next scene.

JENNY SHOWED ALL the dogs what they needed to do in the scene.

"Scruffy? You come running up to Nala and Duke. You've sniffed out where the kidnappers have stashed Cha-Cha."

Scruffy nodded and panted eagerly. "You got it, Jenny!"

Nala barked.

Jenny laughed. "Don't worry, Nala. You get some action in this scene too. You're going to shepherd Cha-Cha out of the warehouse to safety. Fred? Fred?!"

Fred wasn't paying attention to Jenny.

He was staring through grime-smeared street-level windows, looking down into the basement of his old home. The basement where he used to watch *Dog Squad* on Thursday nights. The cellar that had been his jail cell.

Two angry dogs were snarling up at him through the rattling bars of their crates.

"That's him!" yapped Dozer. "That's Dookie! The dog that got us busted!"

"Let's rip him apart!" sneered Petunia.

Fred just stood there, frozen in fear. He recognized the two dogs, of course. From that night in a different part of this very same alley. And what if Big Tony came out the back door?

"Fred?" Jenny whistled. She snapped her fingers. She clacked her clicker.

Fred wouldn't budge.

"Hey, Freddy Boy?" said Scruffy. "Pay attention."

"We're on a tight schedule," said Nala. "Remember?"

"There's a hurricane headed this way," added Scruffy. "I'm a small dog. I don't do so well in gale-force winds!"

The director climbed out of her tall canvas chair and came over to see what the holdup was.

"Jenny?" was all she needed to say.

"We're working on it," said Jenny.

"What's all that barking?"

Jenny looked down into the nearby basement and saw the angry dogs.

"A pair of very unhappy dogs. That's what's been distracting Fred. Can we shoot over the noise?"

The director nodded. "We always shoot the dogs without sound. But can Fred focus with all that racket?"

"Fred?" Jenny held up a treat and tried to get Fred to follow it with his eyes. "I need you looking over here, boy. Ignore those other dogs. Pretend they're not even down there."

Finally, Fred turned around.

"Sorry," he said.

Jenny heard his whimper and smiled. "That's okay. You just need to look this way when Scruffy tells you and Nala what he's discovered."

Fred tried to focus. Tried to look confident and heroic. It wasn't really working.

"Psst," Scruffy whispered at Fred. "What's the problem, big guy?"

"I know those dogs down there," Fred whispered back. "They were snatched off the street because of me."

Nala snuck a quick look down into the basement.

"Don't worry," she said. "We're in luck. Here comes their owner. He probably can't stand all the noise either."

"Ah, shuddup!" Fred heard a man down in the basement shout. His voice was muffled by the soot-stained windows, but Fred knew who it had to be.

"Does the man yelling at the dogs have a mustache?" he asked without turning around to look.

"Yes," said Nala. "Like somebody drew it on with a pencil."

Fred gulped. "It's Big Tony!"

"Huh?" said Scruffy.

"It's my old owner. The man who called Jenny. This is where I used to live!"

"What the heck's going on out there in the alley?" Fred heard Big Tony ask the growling dogs. Next came the sharp scrape of a chair being dragged across a concrete floor.

Fred turned around.

Big Tony was standing on a chair, staring out the basement window.

And he was smiling.

BIG TONY BOMBOLONI couldn't believe his luck.

Fred was right outside his basement window.

"Welcome home," he whispered. He could tell Fred was still terrified of him. Out in the alley, Fred's eyes widened. His legs shivered.

Big Tony spun around to face his two new dogs. Both of them were banging the bars of their crates. "Shut your yaps!" He tossed them some slimy rawhide chews to keep them busy. "My meal ticket just showed up."

He hurried up the stairs as briskly as he could.

Big Tony had been thinking about what he'd do if he ever got Fred back. Shower him with love and affection? Pamper him? No way. He'd cash in on Fred's newfound fame.

First he'd rent the dog back to the TV people. And he'd charge them a ton. Then he'd buy a natty suit so he could take meetings with advertising executives. Fred would become the spokes-dog for all sorts of products, making his manager, Big Tony Bomboloni, the richest dog owner in America.

Whistling casually, Big Tony strolled out his front door to the street. He didn't want to use the back door, which led directly into the alley. He wanted to scope out the situation. Plot his next moves.

"So, what's going on in the alley?" he asked a young woman in cargo shorts with a walkie-talkie clipped to her belt. She seemed to be part of the TV crew.

"We're shooting a new episode of *Dog Squad*."

"Is that so?" Big Tony was good at playing dumb. He had a lot of practice. "I love that show. Can I watch?"

"From here, sure. The alley is locked down."

Big Tony glanced around. He noticed several burly bodyguard types wearing dark blue Windbreakers with SECURITY stenciled in bright yellow letters across their backs. He also noticed a few uniformed members of the NYPD.

He wouldn't be able to grab Fred today. Not without winding up in jail.

"So," he asked the young woman, "what's your job? Are you the dog trainer?"

"No, sir. I'm a production assistant. Jenny Yen over there?" She gestured to a woman with black hair and tattooed arms. She was holding up a small dog treat so Fred would look in her direction. "Jenny's the trainer."

"Oh, I think I read about her." Big Tony was

remembering the Google search he'd done to find a certain phone number. "She runs Jenny Yen's Second Chance Ranch. That's up in Connecticut, right?"

The PA nodded. "Just outside of Wilford."

"Right. Wilford. And that's where the dogs live?"

"When they're not on location. They should be back there tonight. There's a hurricane heading this way. The plan is to wrap early and send the dogs home to Jenny's place."

Big Tony forced himself not to giggle. The friendly young production assistant had just told him everything he needed to know.

Fred would be "home" up in Wilford that very night.

Big Tony hurried back into his apartment.

He used his phone to Google *Jenny Yen's Second Chance Ranch*. Up came a web page filled with photos of happy dogs romping in open fields. Duke, the star of *Dog Squad*, relaxing in his "private bungalow."

"Well, Fred," Big Tony said to the picture. "Looks like you definitely hit the jackpot. It's time to share some of your winnings with me."

He closed the search window on his phone and hurried down the steps to the basement.

He was hatching a plan.

He'd head up to Connecticut and filch Fred in the middle of the night. Security was too tight on the set. But there weren't any guards in any of the photos on Jenny Yen's website. Just a short perimeter fence.

It'd be easy to sneak into the star's "private bunga-low." Once Big Tony had his dog back, he figured Jenny Yen would be much more willing to negotiate. To cut a deal.

To ensure that the dognapping went off without a hitch, Big Tony would take his own security team. Dozer and Petunia. He'd hop over the short fence, open a gate, and use the two tough dogs to terrorize Fred into going for a little ride.

Giddy, he sashayed over to the cages where the dogs were destroying their chew toys, shredding them to pieces. He opened the crate doors to let them out.

"Pack your toothbrushes, boys and girls. We're going on a field trip!"

57

FRED KNEW HE was supposed to be looking at Jenny's treat hand so it looked like he was listening to Scruffy.

But he couldn't help himself.

The dogs in the basement sounded super agitated. It was as if someone had tossed a bucket of raw hamburger meat into their cages.

Fred slowly turned around to look down into the cellar one more time.

The dogs weren't in their crates anymore!

Petunia, the lanky Doberman, was leaping off the floor and banging her paws against the basement window.

"We're coming to get you, Duke!" she growled before disappearing. Then she bounced back up. "We're gonna make you pay for what you did to us!"

"Yeah!" snapped Dozer the bulldog. His legs were too short to even think about springing off the floor. "What she said! We're gonna do that!"

"Um, Fred?" said Scruffy. "We're trying to do a scene here, buddy."

"Sorry," Fred mumbled. "I can't focus."

Nala cocked an eyebrow. "Because of those yapping dogs down there?"

Fred nodded.

"Be quiet!" Nala barked at the window. "We're trying to work!"

"If you two punks don't put a sock in it," snarled Scruffy, "I'm gonna come down there and put a sock in it for you!"

Now Cha-Cha came prancing over.

"What is wrong with you three? I've been waiting to shoot my warehouse scene for hours! Oh, I get it. Fred is holding up production. Letting everybody down. Again."

"Cut!" cried the director. "Jenny? What is Cha-Cha doing out here? And why does Fred look like he's going to be ill?"

"What the heck is happening?" shouted Leo. "Scruffy and Nala aren't supposed to be attacking a window in this scene."

Fred was terrified. His old life was coming to get his new life. He knew it. His stomach lurched up into the back of his throat.

His shoulders heaved. His mouth gacked. Three times.

Gack-gack-gack.

And then he lost his lunch. Vomit splattered all over the asphalt.

"Oh, great!" griped Cha-Cha. "You splashed it on me! Now I've got chunky stuff in my fur!"

Jenny made her way over to where her dogs were clustered. Abby joined her.

"They're all very upset," said Abby, touching her temples with both hands to, once again, amplify her powers of mental telepathy.

"I know they're upset, Abby!" shouted Jenny. "Everybody in New York City knows they're upset! And none of us are pet psychics, not even you!"

Abby looked hurt.

Jenny shook her head as if to clear it. "I'm sorry. I didn't mean that. I'm just mad at myself. Fred can't handle all this pressure. Asking him to become Duke might've been a mistake. . . ."

"You got that right, Jenny baby," yapped Cha-Cha. "You need the real deal. The original Duke, not Fred the fraud. You also need me. You team me up with the *real* Duke and KA-POW. Instant Dynamic Duo!"

"What?" growled Scruffy. "You angling to become Duke's new sidekick?"

"I'd be better at it than you two fleabags!"

"You're out of line, fur brain!" snapped Nala.

The dogs down in the basement were suddenly quiet. Or maybe Fred just couldn't hear them because Nala, Scruffy, and Cha-Cha were screaming so loudly.

He peered through the windows again.

This time the basement was empty.

Big Tony, Dozer, and Petunia were gone. They were on their way to get Fred! He just knew it.

Out on the street, Fred heard a car door open, then shut.

An engine revved.

Big Tony was on the move.

Fred's stomach flip-flopped again. His shoulders heaved. Again.

He threw up. Again.

This time, he hit the toe of Jenny's sneaker.

"Okay, that's enough!" said the director, tossing up her arms in defeat. "We're not shooting a commercial for doggy Pepto-Bismol. So far, this day has been a total disaster."

"I agree," said Jenny.

"Me too," muttered Abby.

"Abby? I'm sorry. I didn't mean it."

Abby didn't reply.

Fred looked from one angry face to the next. He'd ruined a lot more than just the scene.

"Let's wrap for lunch and regroup," the director announced. "And, Jenny? Book your hotel rooms for another night. No way is anybody going home early."

"Come on, you guys," said Abby, leading the four dogs to the camper where they'd eat their lunch. "Aunt Jenny?"

"Yes, hon?"

"First of all, apology accepted."

"Thanks. And second of all?"

"We might need to find a different alley location. This one is totally spooking Fred. I can tell."

Jenny nodded.

She could tell too.

FRED DIDN'T EAT anything for lunch.

He curled up underneath the fold-up table in the trailer and worried. About Big Tony. About Abby. About losing his new family. What if everybody was so mad at him that Jenny didn't even want him around anymore?

"You should eat something," said Scruffy, who had specks of dog food stuck in his whiskers.

"The canned food is turkey today," added Nala.

"Yeah, Fred," cracked Cha-Cha. "You probably need to reload your stomach."

Nala sighed. She was so over Cha-Cha.

"Eat your food, fluff face," said Scruffy. "Leave Fred alone."

When the lunch break was over, Abby and Jenny led the dogs to the new location for the alley scenes. It was pretty close to Big Tony's basement but far enough away for Fred to focus better. He wagged his tail and looked up at Abby.

She gave him a head rub. She knew what had been bothering him.

"Thanks!" he barked.

The new section of the alley smelled somewhat familiar to Fred. He took in a deep sniff.

"Nice," remarked Scruffy, savoring the scent along with Fred. "Garbage. Restaurant-dumpster quality. Day-old meat mingled with bruised bananas. Quite a heady bouquet."

Suddenly, Fred realized where they were. Near the same dumpster where he'd first met Dozer and Petunia.

"Howdy, young fella. Good to see you again."

The old dog Fred had protected that fateful night crawled out from underneath the dumpster.

"Who are all these other fine folks you brought with you?" he asked.

"Um, my new friends," Fred replied. "My new family, actually. We're shooting a TV show."

"Jenny, is that old dog yours?"

"No. I think he's a stray."

"He doesn't have a collar or tags," said Abby.

"Well," said the director, "whoever and whatever he is, he's distracting Fred. We can't afford any more distractions. Not today. In case anybody forgot, there's a major storm blowing up the coast. We need to shoot these scenes! We need to lose the old dog!"

"No!" Fred tried to tell Abby. "He's a friend."

"Lose the dog, guys," Jenny reluctantly told a group

setting up lighting and sound equipment. "He's not one of ours."

Five crew people, who looked like they'd rather be doing anything else, surrounded the slouching old dog. One moved in and scooped him up.

"Now what?" the man asked once the scrawny dog was safely cradled in his arms.

Jenny sighed. It seemed like she didn't want to say what she knew she had to say next. "Feed him. Then call the animal shelter. Ask for Barbara Wolin."

Grudgingly, the man carried the gray-flecked old dog away.

Fred wanted to bark. To howl. But he couldn't. Jenny might send him back. Maybe even back to Big Tony.

So he didn't protest. He didn't chase after the old dog. The director was right. Fred couldn't afford any more distractions or delays. He had a job to do. Otherwise, he might end up in another dog shelter too!

WHILE THE TV crew finished setting up, the director walked over to have a hushed conversation with Jenny.

The director didn't think Fred could understand what she was saying. She, of course, was wrong.

"How much longer until the original Duke is ready to work again?"

"A few more weeks," said Jenny. "Why?"

"As soon as he's better, let's bring him back. We can use the hurricane."

"What do you mean?"

"I've been checking with our weather people. This storm is going to be a big one. Maybe even a Category Four. We'll have to shut down production. Adelaide will put us behind schedule, cost us at least a week. I'll talk to the producers. See if we can have two, maybe three weeks. Enough time for the real Duke to heal."

"But remember our last shoot? Fred was so much better than Duke."

"Yes. He *was* better. But starring in this show, being the lead dog, it's intense. The pace is grueling. It takes a certain kind of fearlessness. Guts. Fred just may not have what it takes."

Jenny nodded sadly. "I have to admit I've been thinking the same thing."

Fred winced. They were right, though. He'd had a chance to show he had the right stuff and stand up for the old dog. But he hadn't done a thing.

"We're ready to shoot!" shouted the camera operator.

"Then let's shoot," said the director.

Fred tried to focus.

But he couldn't.

He was too busy worrying about the elderly dog. How he'd stood by and let the old-timer be hauled away. How he didn't have what it takes to be a hero. How he was probably going to lose the best home any dog could ever hope for.

Fred was so preoccupied, it took hours to finish shooting the scenes that should've taken thirty minutes.

"Um, can we pick up the pace, Fred?" asked Scruffy. "My stomach's reminding me that we should've been back at the hotel hours ago."

"We'll shoot the warehouse scenes tomorrow," the director announced when the crew finally wrapped for the day. "How's the dog playing the kidnap victim?"

"She'll be great," Jenny assured her. "She's a real pro."

"Good," said the director. "And let's see what we can do about getting the original Duke back on the job ASAP. We need a real pro in that part, too."

60

LATE THAT SAME day, Big Tony Bomboloni followed his GPS's directions to a pet-friendly motel called the Seaside Sandman on Atlantic Avenue in Wilford, Connecticut.

Big Tony needed to rent a room. A holding pen for Fred while he and Jenny Yen negotiated terms for the dog's ransom.

He pulled into the motel parking lot and tied Dozer and Petunia to the base of the motel's neon sign.

"Wait here," he told them. "We've got a lot more work to do tonight."

Big Tony hiked up his baggy pants and headed into the lobby.

"Can I help you?" asked the clerk behind the counter.

"We need a room."

"Seriously? Everyone else is checking out."

"So?"

"Haven't you heard about Hurricane Adelaide? It's headed straight for us."

"Hurricanes don't scare me, pal."

"Really? This one should. The Atlantic Ocean is right across the street. The last big hurricane, the one they called the Big Wind, it flooded this whole area. Where we're standing was under three feet of water. If they order an evacuation tomorrow, you may have to check out early."

"I'm not evacuating anywhere just because it's a little breezy."

"Well, if things get really rough, you could take your dogs next door. The Coastal Animal Shelter. I'm sure they have emergency contingency plans."

"Thanks for the tip." Big Tony paid cash for his room. He read a lot of paperback thrillers. He knew not to use credit cards when doing something illegal like kidnapping a dog. "But we'll be fine."

"Can I ask what brings you to Wilford?"

"Strictly business. I'm a dog trainer. Wanted to check out Jenny Yen's setup."

"Her place is just up the road. Not even a mile. You could walk it."

"Why would I want to walk? I have a car."

Big Tony plucked the room key off the counter and strutted back to the parking lot. He untied the dogs' leashes and hauled them to the motel room that would soon become their hideout.

He flicked on the lights.

"This will work," he said.

He turned to Dozer and Petunia.

"Wait here. If you want water, there's some in that toilet bowl. I need to haul the crate out of the car. When that's set up, we'll wait till it's dark. Then you two are coming with me. You need to have a little dog-to-dog chat with Fred!"

AROUND 11:00 P.M., Big Tony's truck rumbled up a two-lane country road.

Dozer and Petunia panted eagerly on the bench seat beside him.

"Here we are," whispered Big Tony.

He doused his headlights and quietly coasted to a stop. "This is Jenny Yen's place. And, if Google is correct, that fancy dog bungalow back there, that's where 'Duke,' the big star, lives."

Dozer and Petunia grumbled at the mention of Duke's name.

"Shhh!" said Big Tony. "Knock it off. We don't want to wake everybody up."

Big Tony climbed out of the car, carrying a leash. It was for Fred. His other dogs wouldn't need leashes. They'd do as he commanded.

"Wait here," he instructed them.

Big Tony scaled the chain link fence. As best he could. Somehow he ripped open the seat of his pants on the third try. After a lot of grunting, he rolled over the top of the four-foot-tall barrier.

"Let's go grab 'Duke'!" Big Tony whispered as he opened up a gate from the other side of the fence.

He tiptoed across the open field toward the cozy little dog mansion. The two dogs slunk behind him.

Big Tony pointed.

"Sic him!"

The dogs took off, tearing through the darkness.

Big Tony jogged after them. For five yards. Then, short of breath, he decided to walk the rest of the way.

Dozer hit Duke's porch and slid through the flapping doggy door. Petunia was right behind him.

"Wakey, wakey!" Dozer barked at the pampered pooch curled up in his nice cushy dog bed.

"What?" said Duke, shaking his head, looking bleary-eyed. "Who are you? What are you doing in my house?"

"What's the matter, Dookie? Don't you remember us?"

"Should I?"

Petunia growled.

"You and me went for a ride together once," said Dozer. "Remember?"

"No. Were you an extra on my show?"

"No, Dookie. You got me caught. By the dogcatcher. In the alley near the dumpster."

"What season was that? We've done so many sequences where I outwit dogcatchers. . . ."

"This was for real! Down in the city!"

"Look, you smooshed-face beast, I admire your dedication to your craft. Acting is believing, and all that. But I really don't remember."

"What happened to your legs?" asked Petunia. "And how come you're wearin' that plastic cone collar?"

"What?"

"You weren't wearing that stuff earlier today."

Duke gave Petunia a puzzled look. "Yes I was."

"No you weren't."

"Was!"

"Weren't!"

Big Tony squeezed his head and shoulders into Duke's doghouse.

"Hello, 'Duke'!" he said with a grin. "Good to see you again, 'Duke.'"

"What?" said Duke. "Who is this man? Why does he keep repeating my name?"

"He's your owner, idiot!" said Petunia.

"Impossible. I belong to Jenny Yen. In fact, I'm her biggest star."

"Well," said Dozer, "from what we heard, you used to belong to Big Tony here."

"Impossible."

While Dozer and Duke bickered, Big Tony reached in

and clipped a leash to Duke's collar. He noticed the plastic cone.

"You been licking yourself again, 'Duke'?"

"Who is this buffoon?" Duke grumbled.

"Nice crib," said Big Tony, looking around the cozy dog quarters. "Don't worry. If your lady friend plays nice, you'll be back here in a jiffy."

He yanked hard on the leash.

"Yowwwww!" screamed Duke. "Hello? I'm injured here!"

"Aw, quit your yapping," snarled Dozer. "Or we'll break your other leg."

"Come on, you lazy lump!" Big Tony dragged Duke out of the doghouse. Then, when the dog wouldn't budge off the porch, he scooped him up and carried him.

"Freeze!" yipped a tiny voice.

Big Tony looked down and saw a feisty little puppy yapping at him.

"Who are you?" growled Dozer.

"They call me Tater! That's short for 'Tater Tot.'"

"And what do you think you're gonna do, tough guy?"

"Exactly what my hero would do!"

Tater lunged forward and sank his tiny teeth into the

cuff of Big Tony's pants. Big Tony, still balancing Duke in his arms, shook his leg vigorously.

"Get. Off. Of. Me!" Big Tony squawked. He flicked his leg sideways.

Tater lost his grip and flew to the ground.

"Grab him, Dozer! We'll take the little dog too! Come on, 'Duke.' I've booked you a room in a very nice seaside motel."

"Why does this man keep saying my name with air quotes around it?" Duke wondered out loud. "I *am* Duke!"

Suddenly, the sky erupted with a flurry of lightning flashes.

The storm was on its way.

EARLY THE NEXT morning, after several hours of listening to Jenny and learning his moves, Fred was ready to shoot his warehouse scene with Cha-Cha.

"We need to work fast today, Fred," Jenny reminded him. "The storm is definitely headed right toward Connecticut. Wilford is going to get hit hard. We need to wrap out of here by noon, head home, and secure the ranch. Okay, big guy?"

Fred grimaced. It was a very queasy smile. *No pressure,* he thought.

Jenny turned to Cha-Cha. "This is your big scene."

"Finally," huffed Cha-Cha.

"I'll be coaching you through the choreography."

"I don't need coaching," muttered Cha-Cha.

"Okay," Jenny called to the director. "The dogs are all set."

"Great. Roll cameras. Leo? Give us the dialogue."

As Leo read the words the voice actors would record for the dogs, Cha-Cha had a few words of her own for Fred.

"Oh, by the way, did you hear? They want the old Duke back. Can't blame them. You have such a weak stomach. Most cowards do. Most failures, too. I guess that's what you are, Fred. A failure. A flop. A fiasco. That's why you were the *F* dog in your litter. That's why your breeder called you Fred."

Fred swallowed hard. "Susan gave me my name," he told Cha-Cha. "She wrote it on my collar."

"And then what? She kicked you out? Just like Jenny's going to kick you out?"

Fred was scared. He hadn't been this scared since Mike told Susan he wanted a purebred. When that happened, Fred lost control of his bladder. In the living room. On the carpet.

And it was happening again.

"Cut!" cried the director. "Why is Duke peeing in the middle of the scene?"

"I think she means the 'piddle' of the scene," joked Cha-Cha.

"Jenny?" cried the director. "Do something with your dog."

Jenny rushed over to have a word with Fred.

That made him nervous.

He tinkled again.

"Tinkle, tinkle, TV star," sang Cha-Cha.

Jenny kept urging Fred to settle down. Abby gave him treats and told him what a good boy he was and how she knew he was nervous because she could read his mind.

They kept trying to shoot the scene, but Cha-Cha kept teasing Fred. And Fred kept ruining the shot.

There was too much pressure. Too much stress. Jenny was right. The director was right. Underneath all the make-believe bluster of pretending to be the heroic Duke, Fred realized who he really was: a coward.

"Leo?" the director called. "Can you get the writers to rework this warehouse scene? Give it to Nala and Scruffy instead of Duke?"

"I guess. . . ."

"Good. Then have them put together something about Duke getting injured. Spraining his ankle chasing the kidnappers. Whatever. Something to explain why his legs are in plaster casts. We'll shoot this scene with Nala, Scruffy, and Cha-Cha and then send everybody home. After the storm blows through, we'll come back and shoot the new pages with Duke. The *real* Duke."

"You hear that, Freddy the Fraud?" Cha-Cha chuckled. "You're being fired!"

Fred slumped to the floor.

"Abby?" said Jenny. "Take Fred off the set. He's done for today."

That was when Jenny's cell phone started buzzing. She glanced at the screen. "It's Mr. Babkow, up at the ranch."

She tapped her phone to put the call on speaker.

"Hey, Jim, what's up?"

"Duke's missing!"

"What?"

"Duke's gone. Tater, too!"

FRED LISTENED AS Jenny asked Mr. Babkow all sorts of questions.

Had he searched the other kennels?

Had he looked in the woods?

Were there any tracks, any clues, any hint as to where the two dogs might've gone?

Mr. Babkow answered "No" nearly a dozen times.

"Should I call the police?" he asked.

"Not yet," said Jenny. "Right now, it's just a pair of lost dogs. I'm mostly worried about Tater. He's only a puppy. He could've chased after a squirrel and wound up lost in the woods. And Duke has three legs in casts. . . ."

"Should Zachary and I make posters?" the handyman asked. "Put them up around town?"

"It wouldn't do us any good. The hurricane is going to hit Wilford hard. The posters would just get ripped down and blown away." Jenny checked her watch. "We're going to shoot one more scene and head home."

Home.

Fred wondered how much longer he'd be able to call Jenny's place his home.

Life was good at the Second Chance Ranch, but it also had to be expensive. Jenny couldn't afford any freeloaders. The dogs had to earn their keep. Fred would be sent to a shelter.

Just like that old dog from the alley.

Abby led Fred over to where the TV people sat in their canvas chairs. He could hear rain slashing at the warehouse's windows. The storm had arrived in New York City.

Fred watched Scruffy and Nala do the scene with Cha-Cha. The scene Fred was supposed to have done.

"Where's your friend Fred?" Cha-Cha asked the two sidekicks when they entered.

The humans couldn't understand what Cha-Cha was saying, but Fred sure could.

"Is he off tossing his cookies or peeing his pants?"

Scruffy and Nala didn't react.

Cha-Cha, on the other hand, kept going. Sure, she struck all the right poses, but she also kept up a running series of rude remarks.

"Hey, did you know that when Fred recites the alphabet, he always skips from O to Q? Where's the P, you ask? Dribbling down his leg."

Scruffy and Nala didn't break character. They stayed in the scene. They did everything Jenny told them to do.

They were true pros.

"Okay, that's a wrap," said the director. "Everybody head home and stay safe. We're shutting down production while we wait out this storm."

RAIN PELTED THE van as it made its way out of New York City and up to Wilford.

The crosswinds on the bridges were so fierce that the vehicle shimmied.

"Look at all that water streaming down the windows," said Cha-Cha from her crate. "You know what it reminds me of, Fred?"

"Hey, Cha-Cha?" said Scruffy. "How about you go bite a bully stick?"

"Settle down, guys," said Abby when she heard the growling in the back of the van. "Aunt Jenny needs to concentrate on driving."

"I've never seen it this bad," said Jenny.

Giant rain droplets splattered against her windshield. The wipers couldn't chase the water away fast enough.

"Will we be safe?" asked Abby.

"I think so, hon. Mr. Babkow and Zachary put plywood over all the windows. We're moving all the dogs to the north kennel. That thing is solid. It's built like a cinder block bomb shelter. The dogs might get spooked, but they should be okay."

"What about Tater and Duke?"

"We just have to hope that somebody's already found them. Or that they'll be able to find shelter and ride out the storm."

Jenny's phone rang. She pushed a dashboard button for a hands-free conversation.

"Jim?" she said.

"No," replied the caller. "This is Tony Bomboloni."

Fred drooped. It was Big Tony!

"We've spoken before, Ms. Yen. You stole my dog, Fred, remember? Then you put him in your big-time show. You even broke three of his legs!"

"I did not 'steal' Fred, Mr. Bomboloni."

"Yes, you did. You stole his personalized collar, too. So I snatched him back. I also picked up a puppy."

Tater! Fred realized.

"But don't worry, Ms. Yen. I'm willing to negotiate for their release. I'll rent Fred back to you for three hundred thousand dollars! Cash!"

"Mr. Bomboloni?"

"Okay. Fine. Make it two hundred thousand. And I'll toss in the puppy."

Jenny took in a deep, angry breath.

Big Tony must've heard it. "Okay. Fifty thou, but that's my final offer."

"You didn't steal Fred."

"I know. I simply retrieved my property."

"No, Mr. Bomboloni. That's not Fred. You stole Duke."

"Excuse me?"

"You kidnapped the original Duke. Does he have casts on three of his legs? A cone collar from the vet?"

"Um, yes."

"That's Duke. The most famous dog in America. A dog you have absolutely no claim on, no matter how flimsy. Do you realize how much trouble you're in, Mr. Bomboloni? The police are going to want to talk to you. The FBI may have a few questions too. Where are you?"

There was a long pause.

"Um, let me get back to you on that."

The call ended.

BIG TONY PANICKED.

Yes, he'd made the phone call to Jenny Yen on an untraceable "burner" phone, just like the kidnappers and spies always did in paperback thrillers.

But Yen knew his name.

He'd have to change it.

He took a closer look at the dog named Duke, who didn't seem too happy to be locked up in a crate, sharing a cozy motel room with Dozer and Petunia. On second glance, the lightning bolt of white fur running up his snout to the top of his head was turned the wrong way.

Oops.

It wasn't Fred. Jenny Yen was right. Big Tony had stolen the wrong dog.

And a puppy. But that was an accident. The puppy wouldn't let go of his pants.

Currently, the puppy was safe. Tony had locked the squirt in the bathroom.

The two dogs he'd brought with him from the city lunged and snapped at the TV star cowering behind the bars of his cage. Dozer and Petunia were howling, frustrated that they couldn't quite bite Duke.

Fortunately, the wind outside was howling even louder, drowning them out. Not that there was anyone left at the motel to hear them. The manager had taken off an hour ago. The rest of the guests were long gone.

It was just Big Tony, three dogs, and a puppy.

And one of the dogs was a TV star *not* named Fred.

Big Tony was in big trouble. The cops and the FBI would hunt him down, rescue the two stolen dogs, send the other mutts to the nearest animal control center, and haul him off to jail. Unless, of course, he moved someplace new and started over.

He'd forget about training dogs. Maybe he could become a chef. He'd always wanted to be a chef.

Suddenly, he heard a wailing police siren screaming up the street.

They were coming to get him!

No. The siren passed. The cops had hurricane business to worry about. They weren't coming for Big Tony.

Not yet, anyway!

He had to get out of Connecticut. Now!

He made up his mind. He'd head south and start a new life. A new career.

"I gotta go!" he shouted over the storm gusts rattling
the windows. "The lady on the phone was right. I'm a
dognapper! I'm in big, big trouble!"

THE DOG TRANSPORT van pulled into Jenny's ranch.

Outside, Fred saw treetops swaying and clouds blacker than any he'd ever seen in any sky—even when *Dog Squad* did their tornado-chaser episode.

"Help me take everybody to the north kennel," Jenny shouted to Abby. "Jim and Zachary already secured all the other dogs back there."

Jenny and Abby slipped into their bright yellow rain slickers and flipped up the hoods. They led the dogs across the muddy field to the cinder block building.

Fred squinted, hoping this was all a mistake. Hoping he could see Tater. Maybe he was just digging another hole under another fence.

The kennel's windows were boarded over with thick sheets of plywood. Inside, it was dry and safe. And packed with dogs.

"Come on, hon," Jenny said to Abby once Fred, Scruffy,

Nala, and Cha-Cha were safe. "We need to go check on the cats."

The two of them took off.

"Welcome home, friends," boomed Reginald. He sat on a dog bed at the center of a sea of dog beds. There were at least two dozen dogs crammed into the space. "So tell me, how was the shoot down in the city?"

"Not so good, Reggie," said Scruffy, finding an empty bed and nudging his head toward Fred.

"We had a few . . . problems," added Nala.

Cha-Cha laughed. "Yeah, problems with a capital *P*!"

Fred tucked in his tail and slunk over to the corner, where he'd be far away from all the other dogs, many of whom were staring at him and shaking their heads. Cha-Cha was right. Fred was a failure. A stray like them who got his one shot and blew it.

He curled up on the concrete with his head pillowed on his paws. Outside, the storm raged on. It was as if the whole world was mad at Fred.

Fred moped for at least an hour.

He also worried about Tater. And even Duke. Duke had been his hero. He'd shown Fred who a dog could be. Well, the TV Duke. Not the real-life one. That one had shown Fred who he *didn't* want to be.

The hurricane battered the plywood boards screwed over the windows. The overhead lights flickered. Suddenly, the whole room went dark.

"Everybody, remain calm," said Nala in her firm shepherd's voice. "Power lines must be down. We might be without electricity for a while."

Cha-Cha whined, "Then how will they blow-dry my fur?"

"Maybe they'll use some of that hot air comin' out of your snout!" said Scruffy.

Fred felt a muggy blast as someone shoved open the heavy metal door to the kennel building. It was Abby. She was soaked and carrying a glowing camp lantern.

"Power's out," she announced. "Aunt Jenny thinks I should stay here with you guys for a while and not bug her anymore with the telepathic communications I'm picking up from Tater."

Abby hung the battery-powered lantern on a post.

"Tater is with Duke," she told the room. "I'm not sure where. There are other dogs there too. Angry dogs. They've all been abandoned. The man who stole Duke and Tater took off. Now Tater's afraid. There's no food where they are. And only one great big water bowl. There are also drinking cups wrapped in plastic. For some reason, Tater wants me to know about the drinking cups wrapped in plastic."

Abby had Fred's full attention.

"But, you guys? I'm worried. Tater's telling me he hasn't been this frightened since a time when a jellyfish almost attacked him on the beach."

No one had seen the jellyfish incident. That had been Fred and Tater's secret. There was no way Abby could know about the jellyfish unless . . .

She really was a pet psychic!

(Well, at least when it came to communicating with Tater.)

"And now," Abby went on, "the hurricane is hitting the beach and Tater can smell the ocean right across the street and he wishes he could run next door to make sure all his old friends are safe because he says true courage is being afraid but going ahead and doing what needs to be done anyhow."

Fred was sitting up straight now.

Tater was talking directly to him through Abby.

It was time for Fred to forget about playing a make-believe hero on TV. Tater was in serious trouble.

It was time for some serious courage.

ABBY SAT DOWN on the floor and started petting Reginald's fur in an attempt to soothe the dog and herself.

Adelaide made landfall not far from Wilford, Connecticut, as a Category Two hurricane, said a news report on Abby's phone. *Adelaide has now been downgraded to a tropical storm. Still, conditions are treacherous, especially along the shoreline of coastal Connecticut. . . .*

Fred scooched across the floor on his belly to where Nala and Scruffy were nudging their dog beds to fluff them up.

"Psst," Fred whispered. "Hey, you guys? Tater is in trouble."

"We know," said Scruffy. "Duke, too."

"Jenny will find them," said Nala. "We just need to stay calm and ride out the storm."

"I can't," said Fred. "*We* can't. We're the Dog Squad. We must boldly do what other dogs fear to do."

In his head, Fred heard stirring music even more heroic than the TV show's opening theme.

"When trouble calls . . ."

Nala nodded. "We know. It's Dog Squad to the rescue."

She didn't say it half as energetically as the TV announcer did.

"Um, Fred?" said Scruffy, looking around to make sure nobody was eavesdropping. "Not for nothing, but we're actors. Make-believe heroes. It's all pretend."

"But does it have to be?" said Fred. "When the trouble's real, why can't the rescue be real too?"

"I understand how you feel about Tater," said Scruffy. "But Duke? Pffft. Why bother saving him? He's never been very nice to you or me or Nala or anybody!"

"Saving Duke is what Duke would do," said Fred. "At least the Duke from TV. We need to become the dogs other dogs already think we are! The dogs I know we can be."

Nala had a very pensive, reflective look on her face as she thought about what Fred had just said.

Then she nodded decisively.

"Fred's right," said Nala. "This is our time to Face Everything And Rise!"

"Ah, what the heck," said Scruffy. "If you two are going to do something stupid in the middle of a tropical storm, then I guess I'm doing it with you. We're the Dog Squad. We do our stupid stuff together!"

"So what's the plan, Duke?" said Nala. "I mean, Fred."

"I think I know where Tater is."

"How?" wondered Scruffy aloud.

Fred nodded toward Abby, who was still stroking Reginald's head in her lap.

"Abby really *can* communicate with Tater," he said. "She mentioned something only Tater and I would know about. The jellyfish."

"What?" said Scruffy. "Was that for real?"

Fred nodded.

"You were there?"

"Yes."

"Did you rescue Tater from that dangerous situation?" asked Nala, arching an eyebrow.

Fred nodded again.

"Well then," said Nala. "When this is all over, remind me to award you the Honorary Good Shepherd Badge."

"They make such a thing?" asked Scruffy.

"Of course they do."

"We need to go to Atlantic Avenue," said Fred. "I'm pretty sure that Tater, Duke, and the other dogs are being held hostage at the Seaside Sandman Motel."

"The one right next door to the animal shelter?" said Nala.

"That's right. Tater mentioned his old friends next door. He also said there were plastic-wrapped cups in the bathroom. That hotel we stayed in down in New York City . . ."

Scruffy's ears sprang up. "It had plastic-wrapped cups in the bathroom! It must be a hotel-motel thing!"

"Exactly!"

"But the Seaside Sandman Motel is what? A half mile away?"

"We can cover that much ground in ten minutes," said Nala, stretching and rolling her neck to limber up. "Five if you two can keep up with me."

"Uh, hello?" said Scruffy. "Earth to Nala. There's a hurricane blowing outside!"

"There's a hurricane blowing outside that motel where Tater and Duke are being held hostage, too," Fred reminded him. "And the ocean? It's right across the street!"

68

"SLIGHT PROBLEM," SAID Scruffy, swiping a paw across his snout.

"There are no problems, my friend, only solutions," said Nala.

"Okay," said Scruffy. "Give me a solution for this, then: motel rooms have doors. We don't have opposable thumbs. We have paws. We can't grasp and turn a door-knob."

"You're absolutely right," said Fred, turning toward Reginald and Abby. "But Reginald can."

"Oorah!" said Nala, sounding even more pumped than usual. "Jenny trained him how to do it for that real estate commercial."

"One of my favorites," said Fred. "The real estate agent says, 'We're opening doors for you!' Then Reginald opens the front door of that mansion with his mouth."

"The guy's good," said Scruffy admiringly. "Real good."

"Let's hope he still remembers how to do it," said Nala.

"We need to talk to him," said Fred. "Scruffy? Can you pull Abby away from Reginald?"

"Easy-peasy, lemon-squeezy."

"Great," said Fred. "Nala and I will go talk to Reginald. Convince him to join our team."

"Wish me luck," said Scruffy. "Although I don't think I'll need it. Diversionary tactics are my specialty."

Scruffy scampered off. Fred and Nala slowly eased their way over to where Abby was petting Reginald.

Suddenly, the room erupted with high-pitched yip-yip-yips.

Abby sprang to her feet. "Scruffy? Is everything okay?"

Scruffy answered with even more frantic barks—the kind that could make even a dog cringe.

"Is it a mouse?" Abby hurried over to see what Scruffy was attacking. Meanwhile, Fred and Nala turned to Reginald.

"Reggie?" said Nala. "We need you!"

"For what?"

"A rescue mission," said Fred. "We need to go out into the storm, head down to Atlantic Avenue, and free Duke and Tater from the Seaside Sandman Motel."

"Oh, do they have a room there? I've always been curious about their accommodations."

"They're both being held there against their will," Fred explained.

"They were dognapped!" added Nala.

"Oh," said Reginald. "Well, that's different."

"We'll have to fight our way through the hurricane," Fred continued. "We might also have to fight off a pair of angry dogs. And we definitely need you to open any doors that stand in our way."

"So, basically, you need me to be heroic?"

"Yes, Reginald. We can't save Tater and Duke without you."

"Wonderful! I've been looking for a way to redeem myself, ever since that embarrassing scene at Pet World. Plus, I owe you one, Fred. You saved my bacon at that ribbon cutting. Now let's go save Tater's bacon!"

"And Duke's!" said Fred.

Reginald looked surprised. "You realize, of course, that Duke would never save any of us."

"It doesn't matter," said Fred. "Duke is a dog in trouble. We are the Dog Squad!"

"Wait a second," said Reginald, beaming proudly. "Am *I* in the Dog Squad now?"

"Today, my friend," said Nala, placing a paw on Reginald's shoulder, "we're all members of the Dog Squad."

"Jolly good!" said Reginald. "But quick question: How are we going to exit this kennel? The door is locked. Abby has the key. And even *I* can't open a door if it's locked!"

Nala grinned.

"Leave Abby to me, boys."

NALA TOOK A running start, vaulted off the floor, and knocked Abby's lantern down from its post.

The light fell to the ground with a thud that disconnected its bulky battery. Since all the windows were boarded over, the kennel was plunged into total darkness. Panicked dogs started barking.

"What happened to the lantern?" said Abby, using her phone as a flashlight. Wind whistled through the cracks around the kennel door. "It's okay, guys. A strong gust just knocked it off its hook."

The dogs barked louder. They didn't love the pitch blackness.

"Hang on. I'll go grab another lantern."

"Scruffy?" Fred shouted over the din. "We go on three!"

"When you say *three*?" Scruffy shouted back. "Or do you count to three and then we go?"

"*On* three," said Nala. "We have to reach the kennel door before it swings shut."

"But," added Fred, "not until after Abby is running up to the main house."

"Timing is everything, my friends!" boomed Reginald in his most authoritative voice.

Abby ran to the door.

"One!" said Fred.

She pushed it open.

"Two!"

She flew out into wind-whipped rain. The door started slamming shut.

"Three!"

The four dogs raced for the exit.

NALA REACHED THE door first—two seconds before it would've closed tight.

She pushed against a fierce blast of wind with all her might and wedged the battered door open while Fred, Scruffy, and Reginald ventured out into the torrential downpour.

Fred led the way into an open field. All four dogs struggled against the swirling wind. Reginald's fur flapped like a thousand billowing flags. Scruffy's ears blew backward and straight up. Nala could've been shepherding cows

through a wind tunnel. It was as if they were all being blown dry in a car wash.

They plodded forward.

"This is when I wish I weighed as much as you guys!" Scruffy hollered. "Small-dog and flying-wig warnings are definitely in effect!"

Treetops reeled. Debris flew. Rain slung itself sideways. It was an absolutely horrible night for a dog walk.

But, with Fred in the lead, the dogs pressed on.

"This is probably what Balto felt like!" cried Reginald, referring to the intrepid husky sled dog who had made the famous lifesaving medicine run from Anchorage to Nome, Alaska.

"Only, he had to deal with blizzards, not a tropical storm," added Nala, her lips fluttering in the blustery breeze.

"True," shouted Reginald. "At least our weather disaster is warmer. . . ."

"If this is a tropical storm," cracked Scruffy, "I just hope I don't get conked by a coconut!"

As miserable as the slashing rain pellets felt drumming

against his eyes and nose, Fred couldn't help but smile as he and the others trudged onward. His teammates were true heroes. No one could make him doubt it this time. Not even Cha-Cha!

"How far have we traversed?" hollered Reginald when the squad of dogs had been hiking for ten minutes.

"Huh?" shouted Scruffy.

"He means how far have we gone," explained Nala.

"Then why didn't he say so?"

"We've made it to Main Street," said Fred. "We need to follow it down to Atlantic Avenue. We need to keep moving."

And so the four dogs did.

CHA-CHA WATCHED THE four dogs slip out the door
when Abby ran off to grab a fresh lantern.

One of them broke that lantern! Cha-Cha realized.
*Knocked it off its hook. That's vandalism. And Scruffy
digging over in the corner and yipping his head off?
That was a distraction! A way to pull Abby away from
Reginald!*

But why did Fred, Nala, and Scruffy want Reginald to
go with them to wherever they were going?

Aha! Of course. Reginald could open doors! He did it
in that TV commercial. They were going someplace with
a door. But why were they going there in the middle of a
tropical storm that used to be a hurricane?

There could only be one answer.

Somehow, the fools knew where the dognapper was
keeping Duke—maybe Tater, too. And it was behind a
door. They wanted Reginald to open that door for them!

But Cha-Cha had to be the one to save Duke! (She could care less about the pip-squeak, Tater. He had nothing to offer her.)

Once Cha-Cha rescued Duke, Duke would be obliged to return the favor and make Cha-Cha a star. His new sidekick. The clever and extremely gorgeous chow chow with a recurring role.

But if Scruffy and Nala got to Duke first, Duke would undoubtedly stick with his old sidekicks because they were part of his heroic rescue team.

Well, Cha-Cha could be heroic too.

Or at least she could take credit for other dogs' heroics!

She quickly positioned herself near the kennel exit. When Abby returned with the new lantern, she'd bolt out into the storm and track down the others. Then she'd overtake them and beat them to wherever it was they were going!

Cha-Cha waited.

And waited.

Finally, Abby pushed open the door. A sudden gust almost blew it off its hinges. The lit lantern swung in her hand, sending shadows leaping across the kennel walls. Wind howled. Rain splattered. The storm whistled its not-so-happy tune.

And Cha-Cha took off!

She dashed out the door. Her ears were blown backward. Her fur coat was buffeted by stiff headwinds. Her eyes were pitter-pattered with rain pellets.

She heard Abby calling her.

"Cha-Cha! Come back! It's dangerous out there!"

Of course it's dangerous, you silly little girl! It's a tropical storm!

But she didn't care.

She had to pretend to be the one who thought to launch a gallant rescue attempt for Duke. She had to follow the other dogs and beat them to the prize!

MEANWHILE, AT THE Seaside Sandman Motel, the original Duke was cowering in his crate.

"Well, isn't this just peachy?" snarled Dozer. "Big Tony runs off and leaves us locked in here with Prince Pampered Pooch. Duke. The big-shot TV star. Turns out he's not so brave and courageous. Turns out, he's a big ol' fraidy-cat."

"Only because I am temporarily disabled," said Duke. "Otherwise, I'd show you two what for!"

Two very irritated dogs lunged at his cage with open jaws.

Duke decided to stay quiet.

He didn't want to upset the two beasts. They seemed angrier than the storm blowing outside.

Duke noticed that his crate had very thin bars. He wondered if the metal rods could withstand a full-frontal

attack from Dozer's and Petunia's massive teeth, enormous heads, and vise-grip jaws.

The bars looked very bendable.

Maybe even breakable.

After a few more growls, the two predators seemed to tire. They both slumped to the floor.

"We've been left to take care of ourselves," whined Petunia. "Just like always. When I was a pup, I was thrown out of the den right after my eyes opened. I never really knew my mother. For months, I thought a friendly rat who crawled out of a sewer grate and offered me some half-chewed cheese was my mommy."

"I grew up eating garbage out of dumpsters on the wrong side of town," said Dozer, sounding sad.

Duke relaxed slightly. His tormentors seemed to be losing most of their fighting spirit.

"I remember my family, though," Dozer continued, staring off at something no one else could see. "I had six brothers and sisters. One by one, they all got homes. Everybody except me. I was what they called the runt of the litter. One night, after my breeder realized nobody'd ever buy me, he left the window to my kennel wide open. It was a hint. He was tired of feeding me and scooping my poop. I was nothin' but a burden. He wanted me to run away! And so I did. I ran away from the only home I've ever known."

Finally, Duke summoned enough courage to try to speak again.

"Excuse me, you two?"

Dozer and Petunia both spun around. They bared their sharp teeth and grumbled up a low, rumbling growl.

"Never mind," said Duke. "I was just going to ask for a little water."

His captors snarled. Then they started snapping their jaws and barking and bashing into the flimsy bars of Duke's even flimsier cage.

"Tater?" Duke cried out. "A little help, please? Come out of that bathroom and save me, young man! And bring me a cup of water!"

Petunia banged her head against the bars of Duke's cage.

"Never mind," Duke peeped.

And then he trembled in fear.

FRED, NALA, SCRUFFY, and Reginald slogged through the storm, which seemed to be losing some of its bite.

The worst of the winds had passed.

But now the streets were flooded.

"Look," said Fred. "There's the motel. About a hundred yards downhill."

The Dog Squad was on Main Street heading toward Atlantic Avenue.

"Seems they still have electricity!" Fred pointed to the motel's neon sign glowing through the murky darkness.

If Fred squinted hard, he could see the ocean on the far side of Atlantic Avenue. Dark, choppy waves, crested with foam, were plowing across the sand.

"That's what they call a storm surge," said Scruffy.

Fred looked at him.

Scruffy shrugged. "I like the Weather Channel."

"As we move closer to the motel," warned Nala, "there's a high probability that one or more of us will be washed away in the flood."

"Heavens," said Reginald.

"We all won't make it," said Nala stoically. "That's often the case in real-world rescue missions."

"Hang on," said Fred. He pointed to a rusty half of an oil barrel that somebody must've been using for a barbecue. It was floating toward them. "Here comes our boat. We can ride that barrel down to the motel. Like you guys did with that raft in the raging river episode."

"My paws were wrinkled like prunes after that shoot," said Scruffy.

The sideways oil drum drifted closer.

"Hop in!" commanded Nala. "Now!"

All four dogs boarded their improvised boat. It rocked.

It almost tipped over. But, at the last second, Fred shifted his weight just so to keep it from capsizing.

They drifted toward the motel. It was much safer than wading through the water.

"We'll have to time our dismount perfectly!" urged Nala, eyeing the surging ocean just across from the motel. "Wait for it. Wait for it."

The half barrel floated into the parking lot.

"Now!" Nala cried. "Out! Everybody out of the boat!"

The four dogs dove into the shallow water just in time! The barrel got caught in the undertow. A wave crashed over it and swept it out to sea.

Luckily, in the motel parking lot, the water was only up to the dogs' elbows.

Except for Scruffy. He was so short that he had to doggy-paddle to stay afloat.

"Hop up on my back," said Fred. "I'll carry you."

"No thanks, pal," said Scruffy, beating the water in front of him with both paws. "I can carry my own weight."

"But we need you to look through that window." Fred gestured toward an illuminated rectangle. "That's the only light burning on the back of the building. It might be where the dognapper is keeping Duke and Tater. All the other guests probably evacuated."

"The window is so tiny," remarked Reginald.

"It's the bathroom," Fred told him. "And that's exactly where we need to be."

"Do you need to pee again, Fred?" Nala asked politely.

"No!"

"Go ahead," said Reginald. "No one will notice—what with the rising floodwaters . . ."

"I don't need to pee!" Fred insisted. "But if what Abby picked up from Tater is correct, he is trapped inside that bathroom. Remember? She mentioned cups wrapped in plastic and one big water bowl."

"The toilet!" said Nala.

"Aha!" said Scruffy. "So you need me riding on your back for a reconnaissance mission!"

"Exactly!"

"Then why didn't you say so?"

Scruffy leapt on top of Fred and held on tight.

"Um, your paws are covering my eyes," said Fred.

"Sorry," said Scruffy. He shifted his grip to Fred's ears.

The rescue team worked their way to the rear of the blocky building. Fred stood up on his hind legs. Scruffy scrambled up his back, the way Fred had climbed up Nala's back in the helicopter chase scene.

Scruffy stood on top of Fred's head and leaned his paws against the windowsill. He swiped away some of the raindrops splattered across the glass with his paw.

"Okay, I am looking down into the bathroom."

"What do you see?" asked Nala.

"A cutie patootie," said Scruffy. "It's Tater!"

"HIYA, SCRUFFY!" TATER said cheerfully to his friend in the window. "Did Abby send you? Because me and Abby have a psychic connection."

"So we heard," said Scruffy. "Are you okay?"

Tater was perched on the lip of the toilet seat.

"Yeah. There's no food, but I have this giant water bowl."

"Ask him if Duke is in there too," coached Nala.

Scruffy turned around to glare down at his longtime partner. "I was going to do that, okay, Nala? I don't need shepherding twenty-four seven!"

"Sorry."

"Ah, forget about it. We're all a little edgy tonight." He turned back to the bathroom. "Is Duke in there with you, Tater?"

"In this bathroom? I don't think so. It's kind of small. I would probably see him if he was. I think Duke's still in the other room with the mean dogs. There's two of them."

"Hang on," said Scruffy.

He relayed the news to Fred and the others.

"We need to go around to the front and rescue Duke," said Fred.

"Or," said Reginald, "we could just rescue Tater and leave Duke to fend for himself. If I might remind you, it's what Duke would do."

"Well, that's not what *this* Duke would do," said Fred. He studied the bathroom window. "Big Tony left the window slightly open. Can you crawl through, Scruffy? Stay with Tater until we open the bathroom door from the other side?"

"Yeah," said Scruffy. "No problem. This opening is just my size."

He dug his claws into the windowsill, chewed a hole through the flimsy screen, and hauled himself through the narrow opening.

"Scoot over, kid," he said to Tater from his perch on the windowsill. "I need to use the toilet."

Tater hopped down. Scruffy tumbled out of the window and landed in the toilet bowl with a splash.

"You smell like a wet dog!" said Tater, sniffing the air.

"I know! Because I am one!"

Then Scruffy hollered up at the window. "Fred? We're secure in here. But I hear some nasty barking in the other room. And Duke's whining and whimpering. I have a feeling he's in trouble!"

"When trouble calls . . . ," boomed Reginald.

"We know, we know," said Scruffy, shaking himself dry.

"Hang tight, Scruffy and Tater," said Fred. "We're going around to the front to rescue Duke. We'll let you guys out as soon as we're done doing that!"

75

FRED LED THE way back to the side of the motel.

"We'll inch along this wall, head to the parking lot, round the corner, and burst through the front door."

"What about the dogs inside?" asked Nala. "How do we take them out of the equation?"

"I don't know," said Fred. "We'll figure something out."

"Seriously?" said Reginald. "That's your plan? 'We'll figure something out'?"

"It's the best I've got right now," said Fred, frustrated with himself.

"Well, Reggie, it's better than anything we've got," said Nala.

"True. Lead on, Captain. Lead on!"

Fred, Nala, and Reginald splashed their way around the front corner of the building. The floodwaters were rising in the parking lot, inching closer and closer to the stoops outside the motel room doors.

"I just hope the front door isn't locked," said Reginald. "I can turn doorknobs, but I can't insert and twist a key. I can't use a key card, either. All I'm saying is, it better be unlocked."

"Oh, it is," said a familiar voice. "I already checked."

Cha-Cha stepped out of the shadows. Her formerly fluffy fur was soaked. She looked like a soggy sock. She also looked slightly crazed in the flickering red glow of the sputtering neon sign.

"I got here first," she sneered. "Nice of you guys to join me, but this is *my* rescue mission!"

"FINE," FRED SAID to Cha-Cha. "It doesn't matter who gets the credit or the glory."

"Ha," sniffed Cha-Cha. "Said nobody. Ever."

"Captain?" said Reginald, turning to Fred. "I really don't want to work with Cha-Cha. She is such an unsavory schemer."

"Oh, you're going to regret saying that," hissed Cha-Cha. "When Duke and I take over, all you'll ever do are infomercials! The kind that run at three o'clock in the morning!"

"You two?" snapped Fred in an urgent whisper. "None of that matters right now. We have a job to do, and we need to start doing it. Turn the knob, Reginald."

"Go on," urged Nala. "Open that door, Reggie."

"Hurry!" sneered Cha-Cha. "Twist the knob, then

move out of my way. I want Duke to see that I was the first one to arrive. You others can just wait out here until he's finished thanking me."

"But—" Fred started, because he could hear the angry dogs growling inside the motel room.

"Shut up!" barked Cha-Cha. "This is my moment. Don't any of you dare try to ruin it!"

"Ohhh-kay," said Fred, retreating a few steps.

Reginald hopped up, braced his paws against the doorjamb, wrapped his mouth around the doorknob, and executed a flawless turn and push.

The door swung open.

"Get outta my way!" ordered Cha-Cha. "It's show-time!"

Reginald stepped aside.

Cha-Cha pranced triumphantly into the motel room.

And was immediately greeted by furious barks, toothy snaps, and terrifying roars!

"Who are you?" demanded Dozer, lunging forward with a fierce air bite.

"Sorry," Cha-Cha squeaked. "Wrong room."

Cha-Cha whirled around, her eyes wide with fear.

"I told you to get outta my way!"

She brushed past the others and streaked across the flooded parking lot, churning up a wake like a fleeing speedboat.

Fred took in a deep breath and stepped into the motel

room. Nala followed close behind. Reginald? He followed, but not so close.

"Hello," said Fred. He wagged his tail, which had that white tip. It was like a soldier waving a *WE COME IN PEACE* flag on a battlefield.

"What the . . . ?" thundered Dozer, looking at Duke, then Fred, then Duke, then Fred again. "What're *you* doin' here?"

"Dozer," said Fred, "I think your beef is actually with me, not Duke there in the crate."

"You brought beef?" said Petunia.

"I believe he's being metaphorical," said Reginald.

"Wait a minute," said Dozer, his face brightening with recognition. "You're that dog from that commercial. You know how to make tacos!"

"Every Tuesday," said Reginald with as much humility as he could muster. "Thanks to Taco Bob."

"And you're Nala!" exclaimed Petunia. "From *Dog Squad*. You're one tough lady!"

"Guilty as charged," said Nala, puffing up her chest.

"Yo? Petunia?" snapped Dozer. "Did you forget we have an issue with this new Duke?"

"His name is Fred!" shouted Duke from his cage. "Fred the fraud. He's the one who ruined your lives, not me!"

"Is this true, boss?" Petunia asked Dozer. "Is this new guy, Fred, the Duke what got us tossed into the slammer?"

"Yeah," said Dozer. "I think so. I don't know. I'm see-
ing double here. It's very confusing. I can't figure out who
to maul first!"

77

"NO CONFUSION NECESSARY," said Fred. "I'm the one who, unfortunately, got you two hauled off to the animal shelter."

Petunia was gazing at Reginald. "I like that minivan commercial, too. The one where you're behind the wheel, doing car pool karaoke with your kids."

"Thank you," said Reginald with a slight bow.

Dozer growled.

"Sorry, boss," said Petunia. "Who are we supposed to be mad at?"

"Me!" said Fred.

"Him!" added Dozer and Duke, both pointing paws in Fred's direction.

"Okay, okay," said Petunia. "Should we tear him apart or what?"

"Not yet," said Fred. "First we need to get Duke home safely. And Tater. He's the puppy trapped in the bathroom."

"Oh, yeah," said Dozer. "I forgot about the kid. He's feisty. Really left some teeth marks in Big Tony's trousers."

Fred chuckled along with Dozer, then turned to Reginald. "Reggie? Can you open the bathroom door to let Tater and Scruffy out?"

"With pleasure," said Reginald.

"No way!" said Petunia. "Scruffy's in there too?"

"He came in through the bathroom window," said Nala. "He's good at that sort of thing."

"I know. I remember that episode where you three had to sneak into the White House to save the president and he was, you know, in the bathroom."

"Hang on," said Dozer. "You can actually open a door?"

Reginald winked. "A little trick I learned for a certain real estate commercial."

"Riiiight," said Dozer. "That was a good one."

"Thank you," said Reginald. "Now, if I may?"

"Sure, sure. Show us what you got."

The other dogs watched in amazement as Reginald grabbed hold of the bathroom doorknob with his mouth, gave it a twist, and shoved the door open.

"Yowzers!" cried Dozer. "That was awesome!"

"Unbelievable!" added Petunia.

Tater and Scruffy came scampering into the room.

"About time one of you lunkheads remembered we were in there," grumbled Scruffy.

"Is Big Tony gone?" asked Tater.

"He took off a while ago," said Dozer. "He abandoned us. Not the first time *that*'s happened."

Fred nodded knowingly. "Not to any of us. I guess we've all been abandoned. . . ."

There was a brief moment of silence as all the dogs remembered how they'd become strays. How some were lucky and found a forever home, while others had to scratch out an existence on the streets.

Outside, the storm was calming down. The wind was barely whistling. Fred heard what sounded like a pickup truck's tires sloshing through the water and stopping nearby. A tailgate squeaked open. There was a splash. Fred tilted his head sideways. He wondered what that was all about.

"So, okay," said Dozer. "You can lug *this* Duke out of here. You, however, Other Duke, you should stick around. We have some old business to discuss."

"If Fred's staying, then I'm staying too!" said Tater.

"Me three," yipped Scruffy.

"I'm staying as well," said Nala. "We're a team."

Fred shook his head. "No, Nala. You and Reginald need to take Duke back to Jenny's place."

"I can't walk," moaned Duke.

"I know," said Fred. "That's why Reginald and Nala will find something to float you home in."

"We can build a raft!" said Nala. "Like in the river episode!"

"Or," said Reginald, "perhaps we can find another floating barrel. That was a jolly good ride."

"Reginald?" said Fred. "Are you able to drag Duke out of this room?"

"No problem."

Duke grimaced. "Drag me?"

"Don't worry, Duke," said Reginald. "I have what we call a soft mouth. It's a gift. All we retrievers have it."

"Come on," said Nala. "Let's head for home."

"On a raft or inside some rusty old barrel?" whined Duke. "No way! You should call Jenny. Have her order me a limo."

"Sorry," said Scruffy. "None of us are too good at making phone calls. Not even Reggie."

"Reginald?" said Fred. "Can you open one more door?"

"With pleasure."

Reginald grabbed the cage's latch with his mouth and popped the barred door open.

All the other dogs thumped their tails. It was how they applauded.

"Bravo," said Dozer. "That was bee-yoo-tee-ful, man!"

"Thank you," said Reginald. "All right, big guy . . ." He grabbed hold of the scruff of Duke's neck and dragged him across the room.

"Ouch!" cried Duke as his head bounced off the floor. "Ooof! Careful, you big galoot. I'm still injured here!"

"This way, Reggie," coached Nala. "I see a floating door. We can use it as our lifeboat. See you back at the ranch, Fred. You too, Tater and Scruffy."

Maybe, thought Fred as he studied Dozer's menacing eyes. *If we get out of this mess alive.*

"NOW THEN," SAID Dozer, prowling in a circle around Fred. "Where was we?"

"Wilford, Connecticut," cracked Scruffy. "My hometown."

"He means, 'What were we about to do?'" said Petunia. "Right, Dozer?"

"Exactly. We need to pay you back for what you did to us, Duke."

"His name is Fred!" Tater offered eagerly. "And he's my hero. You know why? Huh, huh? You know why?"

Dozer rolled his eyes. "Does this kid ever stop talking?"

"Nope," said Scruffy. "He's a puppy."

"Yeah." Dozer smiled. (Apparently, he had a soft spot for puppies.)

"Fred is brave," said Tater, "even when he's afraid."

Suddenly, there was a chorus of high-pitched yelps outside.

Fred heard it first. All the other dogs popped up their ears.

"What was that?" said Petunia.

"Sounded like dogs in distress!" said Scruffy.

"Not just dogs!" barked Dozer. "Puppies!"

"Next door!" shouted Fred. "The Coastal Animal Shelter! Of course. That truck!"

"What truck?" said Petunia. "Did I miss something?"

"I heard what I thought might be a pickup truck a few minutes ago. It stopped. Opened its tailgate. There was a splash. Somebody tossed something into the water. . . ."

Tater scampered out of the motel room to see what was going on next door.

"It's a cardboard box!" he shouted. "Right in front of the animal shelter. It's full of puppies."

The other dogs raced out to join Tater on the concrete pad outside the door.

"Geez-o Pete!" said Scruffy. "Some human must've been evacuating and they couldn't take their pups with them!"

"Either that," said Dozer, his hackles rising, "or they're just using the storm as an excuse to dump their dogs!"

"It doesn't matter how it happened," said Fred. "We need to save those puppies."

"And fast!" shouted Scruffy. "The little guys were wiggling and squirming so much that they knocked the box sideways and off the stoop!"

"It's caught in the current, and it's floating away!" screamed Petunia.

"We don't have a second to spare!" said Fred. "Scruffy? You and Tater go check out the shelter. Make sure there aren't any dogs stranded inside!" He turned to Dozer and Petunia. "Can you two help Scruffy and Tater?"

"Sure," said Petunia.

"No way," snarled Dozer.

He glared at Fred. Fred stared back.

Finally, Fred said, "Please?"

"No way, Duke. I want to save me some puppies!"

"For the last time, I'm Fred."

"Whatever. That box is floating away!"

Fred glanced over his shoulder at the floating cardboard box.

"Then let's go save those puppies!"

FRED SPRANG FORWARD with a splash.

Dozer was right behind him.

"They're heading toward the ocean!" shouted Dozer.

"We don't have much time!" Fred shouted back.

Fred picked up his pace. Dozer kicked into high gear. They splashed and thrashed their way through the water.

They were gaining on the drifting box. But the current was strong. It tugged the floating carton toward the ocean, which, at high tide, had crawled across the beach and was making the far side of Atlantic Avenue foamy with surf.

Fred hoped his legs were strong enough. His heart brave enough. He hoped the same for Dozer.

They swam closer to the box.

Fred could hear the puppies squealing. He could see their bulging, frightened eyes.

"Hang on, little brothers and sisters!" shouted Dozer.

Fred was swimming now. Doggy-paddling. Churning the salty water. His eyes were stinging with every stroke.

"You grab the right flap," he told Dozer. "I'll go for the left."

"Bet I beat you there!"

"Hope you do!"

Now the two dogs raced each other, both gunning for the same target.

The puppies peered over the edge of the open box, their faces filled with fear. Ten more feet and they'd be sucked out to sea.

"Don't worry!" shouted Fred, digging deep for every ounce of courage and strength he could find. "We're with the Dog Squad!"

Both dogs leapt forward and, at the exact same second, sank their teeth into opposite ends of the box's soft cardboard flaps.

Dozer shot out his front paws and dug into the ground beneath the foamy water. Fred did the same. The two dogs skidded to a stop.

They had the box.

The puppies were safe! They started yipping and yapping.

"Baby talk," said Dozer. "Never did understand it."

"Me neither," said Fred with a laugh.

Then, together, the two heroes carefully nudged the soggy box back to the animal shelter and safety.

"SO WHERE'S PETUNIA?" asked Dozer after the puppies were secure on the top step of the animal shelter's entrance.

"Inside," said Scruffy. "She, uh, smashed out that window there."

"She's good at smashing things," said Tater.

Dozer examined the large hole in the plate glass window and shrugged. "Looks like storm damage to me."

"Me too," said Fred.

"You guys?" Petunia appeared on the other side of the shattered window. "I need a little help."

"Did you hurt yourself breaking through the glass?" asked Fred.

"Nah. It's safety glass. Besides, all those years of dumpster diving makes a dog tough. Scruffy, Tater, and me did a quick sweep of the kennels."

"They all looked empty," Scruffy reported.

"Good," said Fred. "That means the shelter was able to evacuate all its residents before the storm hit."

"Except," said Petunia, "I just did another sweep. They left one behind. An old guy. He looked familiar. Says he just got here yesterday. Nobody knew he was in the back. Plus, he was curled up and snoozing in a dark corner of his kennel. I tried to open the door, but hey, I'm no Reginald."

"Let me give it a try," said Fred. "I'm pretty good at imitating what TV stars do."

"Go rescue that dog, *Duke*!" Scruffy said to Fred with a wink.

"Where is he?" Fred asked Petunia.

"This way!"

Fred trotted after the Doberman. The cages they passed were empty. They were also slightly flooded from the storm.

They reached a pen in the farthest corner of the kennel.

Inside, on a watery floor, sat a scrawny old dog. He was so skinny his ribs were showing.

"Well, hello again, young fella," he said to Fred.

It was the old dog from the alley! The one Fred had saved at the dumpster from Dozer and Petunia. (No wonder she'd said he looked familiar.)

The one who'd been hauled away when *Dog Squad* was shooting in the alley and Fred couldn't focus.

"What are you doing here?" Fred marveled aloud.

The old dog shrugged. "Apparently, someone made a few phone calls. Instead of locking me up down in New York City, they brought me up here to the country. So far, it's pretty nice. A lot nicer than the alley, that's for sure. There's plenty of food. Plenty of water, too. Too much water, if you ask me."

Jenny, Fred thought. *Of course. She called her friend Ms. Wolin. She'd had the old guy sent to Wilford! Jenny was a true hero. The kind who didn't need to brag about all the good deeds she did.*

"Hang on," said Fred. "We need to get you out of that cage."

Fred clambered up the chain link door and, remembering what he'd seen Reginald do, locked his mouth on its latch. It tasted like rust. He didn't care. He nudged his head up and lifted the handle, and the gate swung open.

"Woo-hoo!" shouted Petunia. "You're almost as good as that dog from the commercials!"

"Almost," said Fred modestly. He turned to the old-timer, who was standing up, shaking himself dry. "You know, I never learned your name."

"It's Buster."

"I'm Fred."

"Pleased to make your acquaintance, Fred. Now then—

do you folks know where there might be some dry food? I'm starving."

Fred laughed. "Come with us."

Fred and Petunia escorted Buster through the water-logged kennel and into the lobby. When they reached the shattered window, Fred saw a van parked outside in the shallow lake that was the shelter's parking lot.

It was Jenny's!

"I GAVE ABBY a quick call on the mental telepathy hotline!" exclaimed Tater.

"Your human friends have already loaded up the puppies," said Dozer. "Guess you guys will be next."

"You should come with us," said Fred.

"What?"

"You should," said Scruffy.

"But we're, you know, strays. We're also kind of scary."

"Ah, you were never all that scary," said Buster.

"Fred!" cried Abby, rushing over to give him a hug. "Tater told me what a hero you are!"

Scruffy turned to Petunia. "The kid's a pet psychic," he whispered out of the corner of his mouth. "Allegedly."

"We have a connection," added Tater. He hopped up into Abby's arms and slurped her face.

Jenny came over to where the dogs were clustered. "It's so good to see you guys," she said, rubbing Fred and Scruffy on their heads. "We've been so worried. Ever since Cha-Cha ran away and we realized you guys were gone too. But Abby told me that Tater told her you three and Reginald took off to rescue Tater and Duke—and she was right. What Cha-Cha was doing running around in the storm is still a mystery."

"It's true!" said Tater between face licks. "I told Abby all that."

"Anyway," said Abby. "Cha-Cha, Duke, Reginald, and Nala are all safe and dry at home. Zachary and Mr. Babkow are there with them."

"Zachary was the one who found Cha-Cha whimpering by the side of the road," Jenny said with a shake of her head. "Guess the storm scared her something fierce."

Dozer turned to Petunia. "Was it the storm? Or was it us?"

Their shoulders shuddered as they tried hard not to chuckle out loud.

Jenny turned to the old dog. "Sorry about the other day in your alley. We were all a little stressed. Hey, how'd you like to come live with us? I've already talked to Ms. Wolin. I told her I want to adopt you, but, well, the hurricane sort of delayed everything."

"Lady, if you got food, I'm all in!"

"I'll take that happy tail wag as a yes," Jenny said with a laugh.

Finally, she turned to Dozer and Petunia.

"And who are you two?" she asked, bending down to give them each a good ear rub.

Tater scrunched up his face.

Both of Abby's hands flew up to her temples.

"This just in," said Abby, sounding like a news reporter. "According to Tater, these two are total heroes too. They helped rescue that boxful of puppies and found the senior citizen dog, whose name, by the way, is Buster. He was kind of abandoned because nobody in the shelter knew he was back there, all alone in his cage."

Jenny frowned. "Paperwork goof-up, probably."

"Anyway, Tater thinks we should adopt these guys too. Give them the forever home they've never had."

"Really?" said Jenny. "Tater just told you all that?"

"He's right here, Aunt Jenny, so his psychic signals are coming in loud and clear. Their names are Dozer and Petunia."

The two dogs barked in agreement.

"Okeydokey, then," said Jenny. "Dozer and Petunia, welcome to the family. This is my niece, Abby. She thinks she's a pet psychic. And guess what? I think she might be right. Come on, Duke. You're the leader of this pack. Lead everybody into the van!"

"Um, Aunt Jenny?" whispered Abby. "That's Fred, not Duke."

"I know. But Fred plays Duke on TV."

"Still?"

"Hey, if he can handle this, he can handle anything."

"You're not going to replace him with the old Duke?"

"What? Fred's way too heroic to be replaced. Besides, he's family now. And you can't ever replace your family!"

82

EPISODE 3.11
"SMUGGLING SNUGGLY PUPPIES"
SCENE 15

THE OPEN BOX—FILLED with what looks like a fluffy plush puppy—rolls down the conveyor belt in a noisy toy factory operating at full throttle.

"That's not a stuffed Puppsy doll!" shouts Scruffy. "That's a real puppy. That's Tater!"

"They're packing and shipping Tater?" says Duke with a dramatic whip of his head.

"How did somebody make such a major mistake?" barks Nala over the din of the machinery. "This factory is completely disorganized!"

"Well, my friends," says Duke, "it's time

somebody organized it. Dog Squad? To the rescue!"

DUN-DUN-DUN music plays in the background.

Duke hops onto the very long conveyor belt's rollers and slides downhill on his paws. Nala and Scruffy hop on and skate behind him.

There are six boxes between Duke and the one where Tater squeals and squiggles. All the boxes are on their way to a sealing station where a giant hydraulic arm hisses and clicks and closes the carton flaps just in time for a robotic tape dispenser to seal the lid tight.

More robot arms and clasping grabbers will shuttle the sealed box down the line into the cargo hold of a truck waiting outside at the loading dock. Once the cartons are loaded, the trucks will haul the stuffed animals off to who knows where.

Tater pokes up his head. He is trapped in a sea of foamy white packing peanuts.

"Dog Squad!" squeaks Tater. "Save me, please!"

On the *p* of *please*, he spits out a packing peanut.

"Oh, I hate those peanuts!" says Scruffy. "No crunch and zero taste!"

"These . . . boxes . . . are . . . blocking . . . our . . . rescue," grunts Duke as he gallops as best he can across the spinning rollers.

"Hop the hurdles!" shouts Nala.

"Brilliant idea, Nala!"

Duke leapfrogs over the open cartons. So does Nala. Scruffy tries, but his legs are, once again, too short. He ends up landing on his butt in an open box.

"Hang on, Dog Squad!" cries a new voice. "We'll slow down those pesky robots!"

"Look, guys!" says Duke as he leaps over another carton. "It's Dozer and Petunia! The Canine Commandos!"

Dozer and Petunia spring off the factory

floor and grab on to the swinging steel arms. They ride the bucking robots as if they are mechanical bulls. Dozer snarls and grasps a thick cable with his teeth.

"Pull the plug!" shouts Duke, who's just reached Tater's box.

Its lid is about to be slammed shut.

"Pull the plug!"

Suddenly, the robot arms freeze and make a funny DWEEP-DWEEP-DWEEEEEEEP sound as they droop down on the conveyor belt—six inches away from Tater's crate.

"We saved the day!" says Nala.

"Yep," adds Scruffy, hopping into view. "It's what we do best."

"AAAAAND THAT'S A cut!" called the director. "Brilliant work, everybody."

"That's our Fred!" cheered Abby.

"Thanks," said Fred, giving a hearty tail wag.

"That was fun!" said Tater. "Again! Again!"

"Was that okay, Fred?" asked Dozer timidly.

"Perfect. Petunia? You were perfect too!"

"Yo-ho, lads and lasses!" Reginald came flouncing over. "I was just shooting a Taco Bob commercial on the sound stage next door. You should hear what everybody is saying!"

"What?" asked Dozer. "What're they saying? Mean stuff?"

Dozer looked worried. Scared, even.

"No!" said Reginald. "The buzz is—Leo Espinosa is going to create a new *Dog Squad* spin-off called *Canine*

Commandos! Dozer and Petunia? You two will be the stars! You're going to have your own show! On Apple TV!"

"Woo-hoo!" shouted all the dogs.

A tear formed in the corner of Dozer's eye.

"You okay?" asked Fred.

"Yes," said Dozer, sniffling. "I've just, you know, never been so happy."

The crew rolled open the big barn door at the far end of the sound stage.

"Ten-minute break, everybody," announced Jenny. "Then we come back and shoot the grandpa scenes with Buster."

"Come on, you guys!" said Fred. "Let's go be dogs!"

"Only until Jenny needs us back!" warned Nala.

All the dogs trotted in a snug pack out into the open air.

"Hey, Fred?" said Dozer as they walked side by side into the bright sunshine of another glorious day.

"Yeah?"

"Any idea how come I found a plush toy shaped like a loaf of French bread in my trailer this morning?"

"Did it have *oo-la-la* printed on it?"

"I think so. I don't read French."

Fred grinned. "Well, I'm not one hundred percent certain, but I did overhear Mr. Espinosa and Jenny talking. . . ."

"And?"

"Next season, we might be going to Paris! Seems something very suspicious is going on at the top of the Eiffel Tower that could spell trouble."

"So it's Dog Squad to the rescue?"

Fred shrugged. "Guess we'll find out next season."

"You know what else we should do next? We should help all the dogs displaced by the hurricane. They're gonna need 'furever' homes too."

"Good idea, Dozer."

"Thanks. Hey—whatever happened to the other Duke?"

"Oh, he decided to retire."

"Really?"

"Yep. He sits in his doghouse all day, watching videos, eating bowl after bowl of Frosty Paws ice cream. I hear he's very happy."

"Sweet," said Dozer. "You know, we were a little afraid when Jenny worked us into your show."

"But you and Petunia went ahead and did it anyway."

"Yeah. I guess we did."

"That's courage, my friend," said Fred. "True courage!"

"Thanks. But I gotta tell ya—running around like that, doing all those stunts? It makes a dog thirsty." Dozer smacked his dry mouth open and shut a few times. "I'm all out of drool. I could use a big ol' bucket of water."

"Me too," said Fred. "How about we share it?"

"Deal. Where's that water dog?"

Dozer barked three sharp barks.

"Coming, sirs!"

And Cha-Cha, the water dog, bustled over carrying a sloshing bucket in her mouth.

EPILOGUE

MEANWHILE, AT A diner in Tennessee, the new short-order cook was just placing a plate of greasy eggs, greasy bacon, and even greasier hash browns down on the counter when his customer's very angry service dog hopped up on a stool and snarled.

"Hey!" shouted the cook. "What are you doing, ya mutt? Get down from there."

The service dog didn't budge.

"I heard about you, Big Tony Bomboloni!" barked the furious dachshund. "I know who you are and what you did! How dare you abandon those dogs in a hurricane! How dare you!"

AUTHOR'S NOTE

Thank you so much for reading *Dog Squad*! Nothing's too ruff for this intrepid crew of canine crusaders.

The story of Fred, the humble stray who finds himself thrust into the limelight—first on Broadway and then on the number one streaming sensation *Dog Squad*—was inspired by my late dog, who, not coincidentally, was also named Fred.

For eleven years, Fred was my constant companion. We'd go on four walks every day, and he'd help me dream up ideas for new stories. (I think *Escape from Mr. Lemoncello's Library* started on one of those walks.)

But Fred came into our family with a story of his own.

Before we adopted him and gave him his fur-ever home, Fred was a stray, roaming around in the Bronx borough of New York City. He'd been abandoned, tossed out into the street. Fred wound up in an animal shelter, hoping that someone might adopt him . . . and knowing that it might be the end of the road if no one did.

Then one day Bill Berloni, the famed animal trainer who has worked with so many dogs on Broadway—from Sandy in *Annie* to the Chihuahua and the bulldog in *Legally Blonde*—needed two more dogs for an upcoming Broadway production of *Chitty Chitty Bang Bang*.

And so Berloni held auditions and invited all the animal shelters in New York City to send their most talented strays to try out for the two remaining roles in the canine cast.

Fred went. Fred charmed everybody. Fred landed the part!

He went on to star on Broadway for the show's entire 2005 run. His big number was the song "Toot Sweets," all about "the candies you whistle, the whistles you eat." At the end of the song, the tooting sweets attract all the neighbor-

hood dogs. To the delight of the audience, a pack of dogs swarmed the candy factory set, with Fred leaping up at center stage.

When the show closed, my wife, J.J. (coauthor of *Shine!*), who volunteers with animal rescue groups, knew somebody who knew somebody who knew Bill Berloni. When a show closes, he always tries to find his dogs their fur-ever homes (unless it's a Sandy or a Toto—those stay with him at his sprawling ranch for future productions).

We were lucky enough to adopt Fred.

When kids on school visits would ask me about my dog, I'd tell them the story I just told you. And they'd say, "You should write that book!"

And so I did.

Inspired by Fred's wags-to-riches tale, I set out to create an action-packed, funny, and thrilling adventure story about a humble and lovable underdog who rises to the head of the pack and learns what it means to be a true hero.

Because that's what Fred will always be to me.

A GRATEFUL WAG OF THE TAIL . . .

To J.J., my animal-loving wife and longtime first reader, who helped us find the original Fred.

And, of course, to Fred, the most inspirational, loving dog I have ever known. Thank you for always waiting patiently on our many walks when I stopped to jot down ideas for whatever story I was working on. Hopefully, there is no more thunder where you are now.

To Shana Corey, my fantastic editor at Random House, who is always willing to let me chase after new ideas.

To Polo Orozco, a rising star at Random House Children's Books.

To Beth Hughes, whose whimsical illustrations bring so much fun and joy to my words.

To the intrepid crew of copyeditors, Barbara Perris, Barbara Bakowski, and Alison Kolani.

To the designers, Michelle Cunningham (jacket) and Jen Valero (interior).

To Tim Terhune, who headed up the production of this major production.

To our authenticity reader, Crystal Shelley, who helped me get some of the humans right.

And a special full-butt-wiggle tail wag to all of you who have rescued animals and given them a fur-ever home. Thank you for making adoption your first option!

MEET THE SMARTEST KID
IN THE UNIVERSE IN THIS
BRAND-NEW FUN-PACKED SERIES
FROM CHRIS GRABENSTEIN!

Jake spied a glass jar of jelly beans
sitting on the greenroom table.

It was a small jar.

Just enough for one hungry kid.

By the time Emma came back into the room,
the jelly beans were gone.

And even though he didn't know it yet,
Jake McQuade's life was never,
ever going to be the same.

"Chris Grabenstein just might be the
smartest writer for kids in the universe."

— JAMES PATTERSON

"Clever, fast-paced, and incredibly funny —
Chris Grabenstein has done it again."

— STUART GIBBS, *NEW YORK TIMES*
BESTSELLING AUTHOR OF *SPY SCHOOL*

Book 1 is AVAILABLE NOW. Turn the page for a sneak peek!

The Smartest Kid in the Universe excerpt text copyright © 2020 by Chris Grabenstein. Cover art copyright © 2020 by Antoine Losty. *The Smartest Kid in the Universe: Genius Camp* cover art copyright © 2021 by Antoine Losty. Published by Random House Children's Books, a division of Penguin Random House LLC, New York.

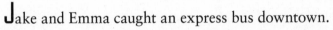

Jake and Emma caught an express bus downtown.

Fifteen minutes later, stomachs grumbling, they hopped off and bustled up the alley that would take them to the service entrance behind the Imperial Marquis Hotel. The building was forty stories tall. Its ballroom could seat five hundred banquet guests at once. The kitchen that turned out all that food was ginormous.

Jake and Emma's mom was in charge of making sure big banquets in the Imperial Marquis's convention and meeting facilities went off without a hitch.

"What's up, you guys?" said Tony, one of the hotel's event staff. He was hanging out on the loading dock while everybody else hustled their butts off.

"Shouldn't you be inside, helping out?" said Emma.

"I'm on my break."

"In the middle of a banquet?"

Tony shrugged. "I don't make the schedule."

"What's the big event?" asked Jake.

"Some dude named Dr. Sinclair Blackbridge is giving a talk to a bunch of brainiacs," said Tony. "Blackbridge is a futurist. From MIT."

"The Massachusetts Institute of Technology?" said Emma, sounding impressed.

"I guess," said Tony with another shrug.

"What's a futurist?" asked Jake.

"A fancy fortune-teller with a bunch of college degrees. He uses science and computers to predict the future. He can tell you what's going to happen in ten, twenty years."

"He any good?" asked Jake.

"Seems like it. I mean, he can't tell you who's going to win tonight's game or nothin', but way back in 1995, he predicted that we'd use computers to buy junk on the internet. Everybody laughed at him. Turns out he was right. Turns out he's always right. He predicted GPS navigation devices for cars before anybody else, too. And those E-ZPass things on the turnpike so you don't have to slow down or stop to pay tolls. The guy's legit. A real scientific soothsayer."

"So, what's for dinner?"

"Chicken, fish, or beef."

"Is there a vegetarian option?" asked Emma.

"Cheese ravioli. Go grab something. We always make extra."

"And we always appreciate it," said Jake. He knocked knuckles with Tony. He and Emma headed into the kitchen.

"Hey, Jake," said a server, a guy named Arturo. "Hola, Emma."

"Hola, Arturo," said Emma. "¿Cómo estás?"

"Bien, ¿y tú?"

"Muy bien, gracias."

Arturo was one of their mother's hardest workers. He was toting a tray loaded down with at least a dozen domed plates. "You kids hungry?" he asked.

"Does it show?" joked Jake.

"We're right in the middle of serving the main course. Go grab a seat in the greenroom. The speaker's done using it. I'll hook you guys up in about fifteen. Cool?"

"Cool," said Jake.

"You want the ravioli, Emma?"

"Sí. Muchas gracias, Arturo."

"No problem. Just hang and chill. We've got that chocolate mousse cake with the raspberries on top for dessert, too."

"Definitely worth the wait," said Jake. "Thanks, man."

He led the way into what everybody called the greenroom: a small cinder-block cubbyhole with a couch, a table, a couple of chairs, and a private bathroom. It was a place where guest speakers could wait or rehearse before they went into the banquet hall to give their talks.

There was also a video monitor where you could watch and listen to what was going on in the dining room. Right now it was mostly hubbub, laughter, and the sound of clinking plates and tumbling ice as uniformed servers whisked around the room with their heavy trays and pitchers of water. Somewhere, probably in the shadows, Jake and Emma's mom was orchestrating all the action over her headset.

"I'm starving," Jake grumbled, twisting the volume knob next to the video monitor to mute the sound. "Watching all those people chowing down in there makes it worse."

"If you were that hungry," said Emma, "we should've just nuked a frozen cheeseburger back home."

"This is easier," said Jake.

Emma shook her head and went into the bathroom.

Jake spied a glass jar of jelly beans sitting on the green-room table.

It was a small jar with a wire-clasped lid. There were only about two or three dozen brightly colored jelly beans sealed inside. A small snack. Just enough for one hungry kid.

Just enough for Jake.

So, since Emma was out of the room, and since nobody had labeled the jar as theirs, Jake popped open the top and gobbled down the jelly beans, one fistful at a time.

They were pretty tasty. Not as good as Jelly Bellys, but definitely Easter basket–quality stuff.

By the time Emma came back into the room, the jelly beans were gone.

And even though he didn't know it yet, Jake McQuade's life was never, ever going to be the same.

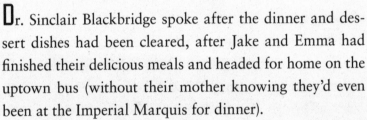

Dr. Sinclair Blackbridge spoke after the dinner and dessert dishes had been cleared, after Jake and Emma had finished their delicious meals and headed for home on the uptown bus (without their mother knowing they'd even been at the Imperial Marquis for dinner).

As Dr. Blackbridge left the stage, he was mobbed by a crowd of eager admirers, all of whom wanted to shake his hand, congratulate him on his genius, have him sign a book, or ask a follow-up question.

One of those admirers was an intense young scientist and inventor named Haazim Farooqi, who had come to America from Pakistan to study biochemistry. Farooqi was only thirty-three years old, but he was a genius, even if nobody (other than his mother) knew it.

"Professor Blackbridge?" he cried out. "Professor Blackbridge?"

The MIT scholar pretended he couldn't hear Farooqi.

"I know you can hear me, sir," shouted Farooqi. "I'm speaking very loudly, and you're only three feet away. The elementary physics of sound waves assures me that you are receiving my auditory signals."

"How did you even get in here tonight, Haazim?" said Blackbridge as he scribbled an autograph in a book a fan had thrust at him.

"Well, sir," said Farooqi, "I'm rather determined."

"And I'm rather busy."

"But, Dr. Blackbridge, sir, I've had a breakthrough! I think. I mean, I won't know for sure until we run a series of rigorous tests."

He finally had Blackbridge's attention. "*We?*"

Farooqi beamed. "Yes, sir. You and me. Together we'll make your most recent prediction come true."

Blackbridge chuckled and shifted his focus to signing another copy of his book. "I'm a thinker, not a doer, young man," he said without bothering to look at Farooqi.

The young biochemist wasn't discouraged. "That's why you need me, sir. I'm a doer. In fact, I already did it. It's done. I left it for you. It's backstage. In the greenroom, sir."

"I'm not returning to the greenroom. My driver is waiting out front. I need to be at the airport."

"But—"

"Call my assistant. We might be able to find some time for you on my calendar."

"No, sir. I already called. Your assistant told me you're completely booked. For the next ten years. Wait. Don't leave. I'll go grab my prototypes. You can take them with you. Maybe do your own research."

"My car is waiting. . . ."

"I know. I'll be quick, sir. Trust me—you don't want to leave this hotel without proof that what you just predicted can actually come true. Not in thirty years. Not in twenty. But tomorrow. Today!"

A fresh wave of well-wishers and glad-handers swamped Professor Blackbridge, pushing Farooqi farther and farther away. One of Blackbridge's handlers was attempting to guide the esteemed theoretical thinker toward the exit.

Farooqi didn't have much time.

He raced out of the ballroom and entered the kitchen.

He dashed into the greenroom to grab his container of samples.

He froze in horror.

His jar of jelly beans was empty.

His precious, one-of-a-kind, irreplaceable prototypes were gone!

Jake and Emma, their bellies full, rumbled back uptown on a city bus.

This one was a local, making all the stops.

Emma carried a white paper shopping bag filled with "leftovers" from their backstage banquet feast: an aluminum tray of cheese ravioli and two extra slices of chocolate mousse cake with raspberries on top.

"Emma, did you know that chocolate was introduced to France by the Spanish in the seventeenth century?" said Jake.

Emma shook her head.

"Chocolate mousse, which of course means 'foam' and not an antlered cousin of elk, has been a staple of French cuisine since the eighteenth century."

Now Emma was staring at Jake.

"Raspberries, on the other hand, are believed to have

originated in Greece. The scientific name for red raspberries is *Rubus idaeus*. That means 'bramblebush of Ida,' named for the mountain where they grew on the island of Crete."

"What are you talking about?" said Emma. "How do you know all this stuff?"

Jake shrugged. *How do I know this stuff?*

"Beats me."

The bus lurched to another air brake–hissing stop.

A family—a mom, a dad, and two kids—seated directly across from Jake and Emma near the back of the bus looked at a map and then at each other nervously.

"Hiki ndicho kikomo chetu?" said the mom.

"Sina uhakika," said the dad, sounding anxious.

Jake smiled. "Unataka kwenda wapi?" he asked.

"You speak Swahili?" asked the somewhat surprised father.

"Of course he doesn't," said Emma.

"Ndiyo," replied Jake. "Ndiyo, nadhani nafanya."

The father, speaking Swahili, told Jake that their hotel was located on West Fifty-Ninth Street.

"Ah," Jake replied, also in Swahili, "then you will need to exit the bus in two more stops."

"Thank you, young man!" said the mother.

"Thank you," said the two children. All of them were still speaking Swahili, and so was Jake.

"Karibu," he said. "Furahia jioni yako yote."

"What'd you just tell those people?" asked Emma.

"I said, 'You're welcome. Enjoy the rest of your evening.'"

"You speak Swahili?"

"I guess. I mean, I think I just did."

"You can't help me with my Spanish homework, but you speak Swahili?"

"It's just something I picked up," Jake said nervously. "And not from Kojo. His grandfather came to America from Zimbabwe, a landlocked country in southern Africa that's bordered by South Africa, Botswana, Zambia, and Mozambique."

Emma was gawking at her big brother as if he were a freak. Jake couldn't blame her. The words tumbling out of his mouth were kind of freakish.

"In Zimbabwe," he continued, "there are sixteen official languages, none of which is Swahili. Those official languages are Chewa, Chibarwe, English—"

Emma cut him off. "And how'd you know all that stuff about chocolate mousse and raspberries?"

"I don't know," Jake replied. His palms were starting to sweat. His stomach felt queasy, too.

HOW DO I KNOW THIS STUFF?

"Are you feeling okay, Jake?" whispered Emma, sounding seriously worried.

"Not really."

"You're sweating."

"Yeah," said Jake. "I guess I shouldn't've eaten the beef *and* the chicken."

"You wolfed down two slices of cake, too. With extra chocolate sauce."

Jake nodded. "I think I gave myself indigestion."

"And that makes you know Swahili, African geography, and the history of food?" said Emma. "Usually it just makes me burp."

"I need to go home and go to bed."

"We should call Mom. You might need to see a doctor."

"No. It's just indigestion. Of course, indigestion, also known as dyspepsia, is a term that describes a wide range of gastrointestinal maladies."

"Jake?"

"Yeah, Emma?"

"You're scaring me."

"I know. I'm scaring me, too!"

GREETINGS AND SALUTATIONS!
YOU ARE HEREBY INVITED
TO READ ALL THE LEMONCELLOS!

Is it fun?
Hello! It's a Lemoncello!

Cover art © 2020 by James Lancett